Southern Craft

A MAX PORTER PARANORMAL MYSTERY

Stuart Jaffe

Southern Craft is a work of fiction. Names, characters, places, and incidents either are the product of the author's imagination or are used fictitiously, and any resemblance to any persons, living or dead, business establishments, events, or locales is entirely coincidental.

SOUTHERN CRAFT

Copyright © 2017 by Stuart Jaffe
Cover art by Claudia Ianniciello

ISBN 13: 978-1543292176
ISBN 10: 1543292178

First Edition: March, 2017

For Glory
Always

Also by Stuart Jaffe

Max Porter
Paranormal Mysteries
Southern Bound
Southern Charm
Southern Belle
Southern Gothic
Southern Haunts
Southern Curses
Southern Rites
Southern Craft
Southern Spirit

The Malja Chronicles
The Way of the Black Beast
The Way of the Sword and Gun
The Way of the Brother Gods
The Way of the Blade
The Way of the Power
The Way of the Soul

Nathan K
Immortal Killers
Killing Machine
The Cardinal
Yukon Massacre
The First Battle
Immortal Darkness

Gillian Boone
A Glimpse of Her Soul
Pathway to Spirit

Stand Alone Novels
After The Crash
Founders
Real Magic

Short Story Collection
10 Bits of My Brain
10 More Bits of My Brain
The Bluesman

Non-Fiction
How to Write Magical Words: A Writer's Companion

For more information visit **www.stuartjaffe.com**

Southern Craft

Chapter 1

MAX PORTER CONCENTRATED ON BREATHING in and out with steady control. He positioned one bare foot forward on the dojo mat and the other foot stretched back for balance. His right arm pointed straight toward the ceiling. With his fingers compacted tight and flat, he focused on the two wood boards set between cinder blocks and slowly brought his hand down, bending his knees in the process, until his skin touched the wood. Everything lined up correctly. He returned to the first position, inhaled deeply, and with a loud cry, he brought down his hand and knees, twisting at the waist, until he felt his hand hit the floor. Only then did he hear the echoes of wood cracking and the applause of those who had come out to see their friends and family test for a new belt in Tae Kwon Do.

Max jumped to his feet, his relief blasting through a bright smile. Master Park, a third-degree black belt, bowed and handed over the broken boards. Max returned the bow, accepted the boards, and sat on the mat with the rest of the testing students.

It was over. He had done well enough in all the sections of the test — forms, sparring, and breaking — and though he had much to learn, he felt confident that he had earned his green belt. Six months since he had started.

As the last grouping of students took position to break boards (and in one case, a girl testing for black belt had to break a cinder block), Max peeked into the audience. The afternoon sun blazed through the large windows of the studio and cast a spotlight on his wife, Sandra. She beamed with pride. It had been a long time since he had seen that kind of happiness on her face.

Usually, they shared a look of either terror or satisfaction that they had survived some form of attack. In fact, after the beating he had taken in his last two cases, she had insisted he start some martial arts training.

"You're never going to last in this business, otherwise," she had said.

She was right, of course. This business — handling cases involving ghosts and witches and supernatural elements — had proven to be quite dangerous. But that was the past. The Porter Agency had to take on other, more corporeal cases or they would find their finances growing too tight to maintain the life they had built.

A series of yells rolled up the line of students followed by the sound of snapping wood and a clunk of broken block. Except one student who had to try three times before breaking his board.

"I'd hate to be that kid," Marshall Drummond said. He sat next to Sandra — floated would be more accurate. Drummond, the ghost of a 1940s detective, had been Max and Sandra's business partner for several years now. Having him attend the testing filled Max with more joy than he had expected.

What a strange life I have, he thought, but the fact remained that it had meant a lot to him for this ghost to appear.

With the testing concluded, all those in the audience walked out to congratulate the students. Sandra gave Max a big hug and a kiss. Drummond hovered above the crowd, not wanting to cause problems with all the people around. A few perceptive folks might notice the cold spot, if they kept walking through Drummond, and that might lead to questions or curious thoughts that Max did not want people pursuing.

"I'm proud of you, hon," Sandra said. "Your mom will be so excited to hear about how well you did."

"Let me get changed and we'll get out of here." He hurried to the locker room, not wanting Sandra to see his face.

His mother had been living in their house for the last nine months while she waited for her apartment to be ready. Of course, she could have chosen any number of empty apartments to move into immediately, but she had decided on the one that already had an occupant. That was it. No altering her decision. So, one more month and the apartment would be available. Mrs. Porter already had her deposit down. It was only a matter of time.

Yet despite the hospitality of boarding her for nine months, despite the constant refereeing Max had to do between his mother and Sandra, despite knowing how much Tae Kwon Do had come to mean to him, and despite the simple fact that he was her son, Mrs. Porter chose to have a movie night with the Sandwich Boys, PB and Jammer J — two teens that worked for Max — instead of seeing him pass his test. As he dressed, he had to wonder why he should care so much. He was nearing forty years old. Shouldn't he be over the idea of having Mommy come see what he could do?

As they left the studio and walked through the parking lot to their car, Max breathed in the fresh spring air. He had his wife on his arm and a good friend floating at his side. That's all he really needed.

Sandra pressed her head against his shoulder. "So, how are we going to celebrate? Wendy's? Mexican? Sushi?"

Max kissed the top of her head. "Ice cream."

"Hey, that's disrespectful," Drummond said. "I'm serious. You can't save the food part until after I've left? Or do you simply enjoy the torture of eating delicious things in front of me?"

As Max laughed, a black limousine pulled into the parking lot. It turned down the lane and stopped in front of Max's car. And it waited.

At first, Max thought it might mean overindulgent congratulations from one of the other student's parents. Or perhaps a loving gesture from the young couple engaged to be married in a few months. But as the various groups of students and families left the building, nobody stopped for the limo. Most looked, though. Everybody wanted to know who it had come for.

"Oh, come on," Drummond said. "You know it's for us."

Max's chest tingled as he walked toward the limo. "This can't be good."

A man in a fine suit exited out of the back and approached with the sure-step of either a politician or a lawyer. He adjusted his glasses with a wrinkled hand before clearing his throat. "Are you Max Porter?"

"You know I am or you wouldn't be here. What do you want?"

"I am Mr. Mane of Howard, Mane, and Jackson. I am the executor of the Will of Ms. Holly Darden."

"Holy mackerel!" Drummond threw his hat in the air only to watch it disappear and reset on his ghostly head. "I think you may have just inherited a fortune."

Max pursed his lips. "I don't know who that is. Some lost aunt or something?"

"A lost aunt?" Mr. Mane sniffed. "Oh, I see. No. This is not about you. Not in that way. Rather, the Darden family is interested in hiring you. They've tasked me with bringing you to their house to help them with an odd problem that requires the unique skills of your firm." He stepped aside, gesturing to the limo.

"Sorry. We're not interested."

Sandra gripped Max's hand tight. "Honey? Shouldn't we at least hear them out?"

"We're not doing that anymore." To Mr. Mane, he added, "I don't care if you've got a ghost problem or witches or whatever. There are plenty of people in this town — heck in all of North Carolina — that'd be happy to take a crack at it for you."

Mr. Mane did not budge. "The Dardens are only interested in the best."

"Come on, Max," Drummond said. "They want the best and that's us."

Sandra said, "That's right. And why do you think you get to make unilateral decisions around here?"

With a lighter tone, Mr. Mane added, "If I forgot to mention it, you'll be well-paid simply for the initial consult. Two days' worth for a drive and less than an hour of your time."

"See? They're even going to pay just to meet us." She leaned up to Max's ear. "We could use the money, and it's about time our reputation got us some work."

Though he still disagreed with the idea of working more supernatural cases, he could not argue with the money. Besides, an initial consult did not constitute working the case. They would only have to go to the house, hear the story, say *No*, and go home with two days' worth of cash. And a free limo ride thrown in. Not bad.

"Okay," he whispered.

Drummond brought his hands together in a sharp clap. "That's more like it. Let's find out what's spooking the Dardens."

As they ducked into the limo, Max said, "It doesn't matter. We're not taking the case."

"Right, right. Stick with that line. It almost sounds sincere, and you might be able to get the lawyer to pay up another day's worth."

Mr. Mane walked to the front of the limo and sat up with the driver. "We should only be about twenty minutes," he said before raising the partition.

The limo pulled onto the street and headed south. Max leaned back with the stench of sweat still on his body. "I'm going to regret this," he said.

Chapter 2

THEY DROVE THROUGH DOWNTOWN WINSTON-SALEM, emerged on the southern end, and continued further down, over the county line, into the rural areas of Davidson County. Max watched as they drove by the trailer park where he and Sandra had once lived. Without a word, she placed a hand on his back and watched with him.

Nobody spoke during the drive. Even Drummond kept quiet.

After a few turns onto ever narrowing roads, they reached an iron gate with two stone gargoyles mounted atop brick pillars on either side. The driver took the limo through the gate and along a winding driveway that cut across large fields and through a few wooded areas. After another curving section, Max saw the house sitting atop a grassy hill.

House did not do the building justice. This was a mansion. A full-on 19th-century plantation mansion. White paint with four tall pillars up front, tall windows and a second floor wrap-around balcony.

"Sheesh," Sandra said. "I didn't know places like that still existed. Unless they were museums."

Drummond said, "They were still around a bit when I was kid, but even back then, they weren't common. I never knew anybody who actually lived in one. Certainly never heard of this one."

The privacy partition lowered and Mr. Mane shifted his body as best he could to face them. "Welcome to Darden Manor. It was built in the early-1800s and mostly used for tobacco farming. If you look off to your right, you can see the old drying barn."

Max glanced out the window. Deep in the distance he saw an enormous barn — dilapidated but impressive nonetheless.

"And those ruins on your left," Mr. Mane went on, "were the slave quarters. This land sits on what was the border of the Moravian properties which made up Winston and its surrounding farms. The original Dardens were neither Quaker nor Moravian, so they had no issues with slavery at the time."

Max stared at the stone walls which once housed entire communities of black people against their will. Based on how close the remnants of the walls looked, he imagined the quarters would have been terribly cramped with more than one person living there. He glanced up at the approaching mansion. Why would anybody want to live on a property with such a horrible history?

Mr. Mane cut into Max's thoughts. "Of course, now all of this is simply land. Nobody's farming it. The Darden kids have other pursuits to follow. I suppose that's the way of the world. You can amass a fortune, build a mansion, create a dynasty, but in the end, you can't control what your children will do with it all. And, of course, times have changed, so perhaps they don't view an old plantation like this with the reverence that many others still hold." With a twinkle in his eye, he covered his mouth. "Oh, listen to me, yakking on. It's just that I had a great fondness for Ms. Darden, and it was a shame to see her pass."

The limo stopped, but before they got out, Sandra asked, "How exactly did that happen?"

"Nothing nefarious, if that's what you're implying. She always had a troublesome heart, and though young — she was only fifty-seven — she went into cardiac arrest. She was driving to the doctor for a checkup, of all things."

Mr. Mane scooted out of the limo and led the way up to the wide stairs of the front porch. The closer they came to the main door, the more the lawyer began to shake. The smile plastered on his face trembled, and his eyes darted around as if searching for a threat behind every bush or tree.

"Well, then," he said, sweat beading on his face. "Here we are. When you're ready to leave, the car will be here to take you home. My offices will be in contact to arrange payment for your services today."

Max said, "You're not coming in?"

"No." Mr. Mane exhaled and chuckled at the same time. "No, no, no. I have many important matters to attend to before the day is over. Don't worry, now. The limo driver has explicit orders to wait here for you. Even after the sun goes down. Good day."

As Mr. Mane hustled down the drive and around the side of the house, Drummond tipped back his hat and shook his head. "Nothing suspicious about any of that. Geez."

Max shot a look up at the ghost, but before he could comment, Sandra rang the doorbell — a deep, two-toned ring that echoed in the stately home.

"See anything?" Max asked Sandra.

Though Max had no trouble seeing Drummond, he could not tune in any other ghosts. Sandra, on the other hand, had a real knack for it. She saw all the ghosts.

Making a quick survey around them, she nodded off toward some fields. "Looks like some ghosts of slaves are back there. Otherwise, things are quiet."

They heard the steady click of heels and then the large door opened. A woman stood there, relief and fear battling across her round face. She wore a black dress and pearls.

Hints of gray dappled her dark hair. "Ah, you must be the Porters. Thank you for coming." She stepped back to let them in before extending a gloved hand. "I'm Chelsea Darden. We appreciate any help you can offer."

Max shook the hand, surprised by her firm grip, and said, "We're here for an initial consult and nothing more. We've not officially taken the case."

"I understand. Still, just being heard is going to be a blessing."

They stood in an enormous foyer. The ceiling rose two stories and a stained-glass dome colored the late-day sunlight dripping in. The floor had been made of old stone and a circular area rug covered the center. A marble staircase that curved its way up to the second floor drew Max's attention. It had an elegant yet dark feel to it — mostly due to the hunched gargoyle sitting at the front end of the heavy-wood banister.

Chelsea must have been watching him for she answered his unspoken question. "Aunt Holly did love some macabre things. Especially the gargoyles. But at least she enjoyed bright, cheery things, too." She gestured to a waist-high table by the door. On it, Max saw a basket for mail and an ornate letter opener. Two porcelain figures of dancing bears stood on either side of the basket.

"It's a lovely home," Sandra said.

"Thank you. It's going to be mine soon. I'll have to decide about all the little details from now on." Chelsea stared at the gargoyle. "That'll have to go. Maybe we'll keep a couple around in memoriam." She flustered. "Oh, my, I must sound awful. It's just that, well, this has been a terribly trying time for us. Aunt Holly's passing was so unexpected."

"I'm sure. The lawyer said she was quite young."

"We all thought she'd be around for another twenty

years, at least. I wish she was because she'd know how to handle this situation. Please, follow me and I'll explain everything."

As they headed through a wide archway, Drummond could not hold back a gleeful snicker. "I'm telling you, I have a good feeling about this one. Especially the money. You guys are going to pull in a year's worth of cash on this case."

Max tensed but kept quiet.

They entered a living room that mixed modern and antique furnishings. Old-style couches and reading chairs had been artfully placed upon Turkish rugs while a flatscreen television had been mounted on the wall and small, high-powered speakers could be spotted in the corners of the room near the ceiling. A low coffee table with carved legs held a vase with a bouquet of lilies. Another porcelain figure — this one of a bear in a tutu lying on its back — rested next to the flowers.

A teenage girl looking like a youthful version of Chelsea had one leg propped on the back of the couch while the rest of her stretched out with her head hanging slightly off the side. She held a tablet and bopped her head to the music blaring in her earbuds — loud enough for Max to hear the steady drums and an occasional guitar. She did not seem to notice Max and the others.

On the other side of the room, a small card table had been set up near an empty fireplace. An elderly woman in a wheelchair sat on one side, a man near the same age as Chelsea sat at the other, and a wooden cribbage board sat between them. The rail-thin, balding man seemed uninterested in the game — probably because the old woman looked catatonic.

Chelsea stopped in the center of the room and gestured to the man. "This is my older brother, Alan."

Barely lifting his head, Alan said, "Hi."

"Don't be sullen," Chelsea said before gesturing toward the old woman in the wheelchair. "This lovely lady is Grandma Darden. She's ninety-seven years old. Can you believe it? Still strong as ever."

Grandma Darden turned her head toward Max with a desperate look in her eye as if to say, *I'd rather be dead than have to put up with Miss Cheery for another day.* Max suppressed a laugh and merely nodded at the woman. The woman continued to stare, and Max wondered if she saw him at all or if that look in her eye was merely the confused look of dementia.

Sandra may have caught the unspoken conversation because she swiftly turned Chelsea's attention toward the teenager. "This must be your daughter."

Chelsea giggled. "Oh, no, not at all. That's Lane. She's our younger sister." With a whisper, though Lane could not possibly hear anything other than heavy bass and drums, Chelsea added, "An unexpected gift to my parents."

Walking onward, she waved for Max and Sandra to follow. As they left, Max caught Lane watching them leave. She scowled. Maybe she could read lips.

A carpeted hall ate up most of the sound as they headed toward cherry wood double-doors. Chelsea pushed both doors open, and they entered a large library. The Darden family certainly enjoyed books. The library had a mythical quality with a vaulted wood ceiling, a second story of bookshelves only accessible via a rolling ladder, and a massive paned window that overlooked the endless fields. Three aisles on either side of the room housed more books and all of it had been designed to draw the eye toward the center of the room where Chelsea sat behind a desk clearly made from the stump of a fallen oak.

Drummond whistled as he flew up to inspect the books

near the top. "What is it with rich folk and libraries? It's like they think the commoners will assume they've actually read all these books. I'm sorry but no way did any of the people living here get all excited to read ..." He cocked his head to the side as he looked upon one title. "... *Variations in Rodent Scat.* Really?"

"Please," Chelsea said, gesturing to high-backed chairs in front of the desk.

Max and Sandra settled in. After noticing how Chelsea's hands shivered, Max watched her lace her fingers tight as she forced a faux-calm expression.

"Now," she said, her voice cracking at first, "I hope you understand that discretion is expected. My family has never wanted to be in the spotlight and I would be upset if that changed."

Sandra said, "Have no worries. We keep all our client information strictly confidential."

"Though," Max said, "keep in mind that you are not our clients yet. However, since you have paid for this consult, I suppose we will consider anything you say today to be confidential even if we don't take your case."

"That seems fair," Chelsea said, her eyes shifting from Max to Sandra and back.

For Max's part, he had no need to look at Sandra. He could feel the fire in his side burning from her glare.

Chelsea straightened in her chair. "I'm sure Mr. Mane informed you that this has to do with the Will of my Aunt Holly. She was a fine woman. She meant everything to us. She raised us. And took care of Grandma Darden, too."

"Hey," Drummond said as he lowered to the floor. "Ask her about her husband. Where is the guy?" Max glanced at Drummond and the ghost said, "Come on. Surely you noticed the rock on her finger."

Max had to admit he forgot to look. This whole meeting

had annoyed him to the point of failing the basics Drummond had taught him. But he also had no interest in asking questions.

Sandra, however, wasted no time. "How long have you been married?"

Stretching her hand out to gaze upon her ring, Chelsea's face warmed. "Not a single day, yet. Enrique proposed four months ago. We were going to set a wedding day soon, but now that Aunt Holly passed, we haven't had time to deal with it. Yet."

"Your parents must be proud."

She lowered her head as if praying for strength, and then inhaled sharply. "My parents died shortly after Lane was born. They were driving to a pet store, of all places, to look for a puppy. I think they worried how Alan and I might feel with this late addition to the family. But I was in college and Alan was about to graduate. We didn't care. It was winter, and the usual North Carolina ice storms had hit. They lost control of the car and slid right off the road. The car was old and only had an airbag for the driver, so my mother died right away when they smashed into a tree. My father hit the airbag at an odd angle. It broke his glasses and knocked him unconscious, bending his head in such a way that he could not get enough air to adequately breathe. By the time the rescue teams had arrived, he had died as well."

"I'm sorry," Sandra said. "That sounds awful."

"Thank you, but there's no need. It was long ago. At the time, though, it was devastating. Both Alan and I dropped out of school. We weren't well off, and we had no idea what to do with a baby. Luckily, Aunt Holly came to our aid. This home belonged to her. She took us in. She home-schooled Lane, and helped Alan and I cope with our loss." Chelsea paused again as if searching for words that would never come. "When Grandma Darden grew ill, Aunt Holly brought her to this house as well. She was there for all of us. In a way, her death has been far worse a blow to this family than losing our parents. Especially for Lane. She was too little to remember Mom and Dad, but Aunt Holly was her whole world."

Max said nothing. He wondered how much of this sob story was true. Certainly Lane did not look like a girl whose whole world had been ripped away.

Sandra must have sensed some of this, too, because she said, "You didn't ask us here to handle a typical family death. That's what your lawyer is for. So, why not spit it out? You'll feel better, and I promise we won't doubt you. We've seen a lot of strange things in our line of work."

"Of course. My apologies. I wasn't trying to stall. It's simply not every day I have to talk about such things. It's uncomfortable." Another deep breath, and Chelsea spoke. "Shortly after Aunt Holly passed away, a man came to our door. I remember this so clearly. It had been an emotionally exhausting time with the funeral and all, and I had gone up to my bedroom. I had put my head down to rest when I heard Alan arguing with this man. Before I even got to the front door, I was yelling that I'd call the police. He ran off to his car and left. I didn't get a good look at him, but Alan did. He said the man wore a gray suit and dark blue tie. The man said that Aunt Holly had destroyed his life and he would never forgive us for it. He said that we were her family and we deserved to be punished as did our children and so on for ten generations. He also said that this house was built on the pain and suffering of others, that all our fortunes past and present were at the expense of others. He said that since we loved this place so much, we would never leave here again. He then painted a symbol on one of the outside pillars before running off." She dabbed at the tear running down her cheek. "Ever since then, we've been trapped."

"Trapped?" Sandra asked.

"All four of us are stuck in the house. We can't leave. Alan tried and suffered tremendous pain. He dared to step on the porch — just the porch — and the pain doubled him over. By the time he got back inside, the skin on his arms had reddened like a sunburn — except this happened at night. We are stuck here by that man's spell."

Though he didn't want to encourage this conversation any further than necessary, Max had a suspicion he wanted confirmed. "This man said your Aunt Holly had destroyed his life, and you mentioned that he used a spell. Based on the casual way you referred to magic, and the fact that you specifically sought us out, I'm guessing your aunt was a witch."

"Oh, certainly." Chelsea walked over to a shelf at the right and returned with a photo album. She opened to an old black and white photograph with the edges cut in tiny waves. A girl, no more than eight years old, stood in front of a mule in the middle of a large field. "That was Aunt Holly in 1948. Look here." She pointed at a charm bracelet around the girl's wrist.

"It's hard to see," Sandra said, "but I think some of those are wards."

"That's correct. The Darden women have been handing down the secrets of magic for centuries. All the way back to our ancestors in Germany. We were never particularly accomplished at it. We were smart not to dabble too deeply for fear of falling into the dark fathoms of witchcraft, but we knew enough to recognize that such a world existed."

Max bristled at the thought of his wife's dabbling. Sandra had been studying witchcraft more and more. It was becoming an obsession, but anytime he broached the idea that she should consider backing off a little, he was met with firm resistance.

"The problem," Chelsea continued, "is that sometimes these minor little spells have tangential effects. At least, that's what I think happened. Aunt Holly tried to get me interested, but I've managed to stay as far away from this stuff as possible. I suspect she cast a spell at some point meant to help in a minor way — perhaps get me a date to my senior prom or something equally benign — when the whole thing backfired."

Sandra nodded. "You think this man with the blue tie got caught by the *tangential effects?*"

"Maybe. He certainly thinks so. I'm not sure what happened to him, but clearly he's angry and taking it out on us. Except the kind of magic he's using is serious. I mean, we're not going to starve to death. We get food brought in as needed. But we can't live the rest of our lives here. And, quite frankly, I don't think he's done with us. My guess is that he is planning some way of stealing all of Aunt Holly's money. He wants to ruin us."

"And you want us to stop him."

Chelsea paled. "Oh. No. We contacted you because you both have become well-known in this area. Our meager knowledge of magic is no match for this man. We hoped you might be able to break the spell and set us free. Going after the man wasn't something we had considered. Do you do that sort of thing — vengeance?"

With a distasteful grimace, Max folded his arms. "We're not contract killers."

"Forgive me. I didn't mean to suggest that. I only meant that I wondered if you could track this man down, find out why he ... well, none of that matters. The important thing is to free us from this spell. We can handle the rest after that."

Drummond soared in close. "Finally, a good case has come our way. The last bunch of months have been so boring, I thought all the witches had given up."

From the corner of his eye, Max saw Sandra lean forward and smile. Before she could say a word, he blurted out, "No. I'm sorry, but we're not getting involved with these kinds of cases anymore."

Chelsea's face dropped. "Please. You have to."

"Partner," Drummond said, "what are you doing?"

Max stood. "Thank you for considering us, but I'm afraid we can't help you." He turned and headed out the door.

Placing a hand on his sleeve, Sandra sent him a confused look with anger simmering underneath, but he kept moving. The shocked silence that followed in his wake lasted only a few seconds. With a shaking cry, Chelsea rushed around her desk.

"Please, Mr. Porter. It's important that you help us. Nobody else can do this."

Max entered the living room. All eyes lifted to him. Even Lane set aside her social media addiction long enough to notice.

"We'll pay you double," Chelsea said, bursting into the room.

Max turned around to decline once more when he saw her lock eyes with Alan. Then her gaze shifted to Lane. With an embarrassed smile, she straightened her hair and adjusted her dress. In a calmer voice, she added, "Upfront. We'll pay you upfront."

Drummond slipped through the wall. "C'mon, that's a great deal. When have we ever gotten full payment before the case even started?"

Max put out his hand and waited for Chelsea to take it. "I'm sorry, Ms. Darden. I wish you the best, but the answer is still no."

As he turned toward the foyer, Chelsea dropped to her

knees. She clasped her hands and cried out, "Please. I beg you. Please don't leave us at the mercy of this spell."

He stopped and looked back. Part of him wanted to scoop up the terrified woman and let her know that they would take care of it all. They had the experience. They could handle it. But another part reminded him of the cost for all that experience. How many more times could they tempt Death?

Listening to Chelsea sob, Max fought down the idea that he was a horrible human being. He couldn't save everybody, and certainly, no one would deny him the right to save his own family first. But when he stepped closer to gently tell Chelsea a final *No*, he caught a sad gaze cross the room from Grandma Darden to Sandra.

Sandra's hand went to her chest as she said, "Maybe. We can't promise anything, but we can take a little time to investigate what's going on." Catching Max clamp his mouth tight, she added, "Even if we don't take the case, we'll find somebody to refer you to. We know plenty of people who use magic that might be able to help."

"Oh, thank you," Chelsea said, and her relief threatened to bring another round of sobs. With a hand from Alan, she got back on her feet and hurried to the front door. "You won't regret this. I have full faith in you. Thank you again."

I already regret this, Max thought but only reminded her that they had not agreed to take the case — only to look into it.

Sandra added, "Don't worry. I promise we'll contact you soon with whatever decision we make."

Chelsea leaned on the door and watched as Max and Sandra ducked into the waiting limousine. Max knew she would remain standing there until she could no longer see the headlights shine across the trees and fields. Even after he assumed she had gone inside, after the limo had cruised under the gargoyle gate and headed onto the main roads, Max felt as if she continued to watch them.

No matter. Sandra and Drummond could argue all they wanted. Max had no intention of taking this or any other case involving witches and magic. Not ever again.

Chapter 3

NOBODY SPOKE THROUGHOUT THE RIDE BACK to the Tae Kwon Do parking lot. Nobody spoke throughout the ride home. Not even Drummond.

Max knew an argument was inevitable. The fact that his mother still resided at their home only made it worse. She would be listening, possibly commenting, and no matter the outcome, she would feel it necessary to offer a point of advice. Or two.

As they pulled off Silas Creek Parkway and headed into the neighborhood of nice homes and manicured lawns, he slumped in his seat. Keeping the money flowing so that they could enjoy a big house and a fancy yard exhausted him with constant worry. Yet their life prior to their windfall had been no better. Instead of yard services and hefty tax bills, he had spent those years worrying about finding enough money for food or heat. The categories had changed, but the worry remained.

Yet one thing he had learned through all their battles with the Hull family, the witches and ghosts, the power-hungry and the downtrodden — no amount of money would be worth selling out.

Stepping into the house, Max found his mother cleaning up from the movie night with PB and Jammer J. The Sandwich Boys had fallen for Mrs. Porter hard. Why wouldn't they? She showered them with the kind of motherly love and doting they had never received before. Thankfully, they had returned to their apartment — Max didn't need them taking sides in the coming argument.

Sandra wasted no time. Before she had removed her coat, she said, "What's the matter with you?"

Drummond jumped in. "I second that. This is a good deal. The best we've ever seen."

"It's only a good deal," Max said, "if we want to get ourselves in trouble again."

Clearing away a few glasses, Mrs. Porter scurried into the kitchen. But Max was not fooled. Her haste had nothing to do with getting out of the way and everything to do with finishing up quickly so she could return fast.

"Are you kidding me?" Drummond said. "You run a detective agency. Every case is about some sort of trouble. The fact that this agency specializes in magic-related cases only doubles things."

"That's my point. These cases get more and more dangerous. Did you notice the shape I was in after the last time?"

Sandra closed her eyes and took a breath before approaching in a nicer tone. "Honey, I understand that you had a rough time —"

"A rough time. I had three broken ribs. I'm lucky I didn't have a punctured lung."

"But that's why you took up martial arts. Isn't it?"

"I want to be able to protect myself. That doesn't mean I should go looking for trouble. Hell, I was in a coma earlier this year and nearly died."

A glass clattered in the kitchen sink. "What?" Mrs. Porter said, stomping back to the living room.

"Look," Max said, "we've been dealing with these crazy cases ever since we moved down here, and I'm done with it. All we ever do is put ourselves on the line, and then we've got to fight to get paid anything. Let's cool it for a bit. Let's take some normal, boring cases. The kind where I go to the library and do the research and then it's over.

Nobody shooting at us. Nobody delving into magic. None of it."

Drummond clicked his tongue. "You wouldn't last a week doing that. Maybe when you first moved here, but not anymore. Danger is part of this job, but it's part of the rush, too. You know it."

"No, thank you."

With one hand on her hip and the other stabbing in his direction, Sandra dropped her calm demeanor. "Look here. You don't get to decide for all, and you don't get to back out of something we've built together. I'm talking about us, in case you're too thick-headed to understand."

"Us? What does this —"

"Don't you dare finish that sentence. You know exactly what's going on here and how making a decision like that impacts us both."

Drummond snapped his fingers. "Me, too."

"We have bills," Sandra went on. "We have old debt. We have people who count on us to be earning a living. Or do you think PB and J are simply going to get another job somewhere else when we fold because we stop taking all the cases we're good at?" Max tried to answer, but Sandra's stabbing finger raised upward to silence him. "We need the money. Plain and simple. And these cases are what we do. They tap into our skills more than anything else we've ever done. And you know this to be true — we're better at it than anybody else around here."

"I'm not changing my mind. Especially not for the Dardens. For crying out loud, you heard them. You think breaking some spell so they can claim an inheritance unencumbered is going to go smoothly? Look how that woman threw herself on the ground for us. Tell me that was normal. She was so desperate that you know there had to be more to this story. The mystery man coming out of nowhere to curse them? Come on."

"So what? We'll figure it out. We always do. Besides, are you really going to start turning your back on people in need? Is that the kind of man you've become? Because you know that's not the kind of man I want. Don't even make me start going down that road of conversation."

Max waited to make sure she had finished. "I know we need the money to keep flowing. I'm not an idiot." He glared at Drummond, daring the ghost to make a comment. "Everything you said about us being the best and the rush of the work and helping people, all of it — it's true. And that was wonderful when it was just us. But now there's my mom and the Sandwich Boys. You said it yourself, they depend on us. You wonder what'll happen to them if we stop making money. What's going to happen to all of you if I end up dead? Or worse?"

Mrs. Porter's face reddened as she slammed her hand against the wall to get everyone's attention. "You almost died?"

Max flailed his arms at Sandra. "Ask her," he said and stormed through the kitchen to his study. He slammed the door shut and slumped in his desk chair. Drummond flew through the wall, and Max flung a pencil at him. "I would've thought a smart detective like you understood that slamming the door meant I didn't want to talk anymore."

"Listen, pal, you're screwing this whole thing up, and when it all comes down, you'll still end up apologizing to your sweet wife."

"Gee, thanks, you're being a real swell guy."

"I'm your friend. Sometimes that means telling you when you're acting like an ass."

"Why am I an ass for wanting to keep us all safe?"

"You've got it all twisted up in your head." Drummond

slid into a chair next to the desk. He took off his hat and tapped the brim against his knee. When he finally looked at Max, his dead eyes sparked with intensity, but his voice remained cold and clear. "I understand. I do. The last six months, you haven't had a case, nobody threatening your life, and you've started thinking how that feels. Let's face it — it feels pretty good. But it won't last."

"I'm not saying we'll never do another magic case."

"It's what you want to say. But if you listen to me, I'm telling you —"

"What? What is it that you're so eager to tell me?"

"You need to hear about my case with the Dega Witch. The worst case I ever had."

Chapter 4

BEFORE DRUMMOND COULD BEGIN, there came a knock at the door. "Max?" his mother's muffled voice called.

A moment later, he heard Sandra shoo his mother away. "Let him be. He needs to cool off."

No matter what else Drummond would say that night, he had been right about one thing — Max would have to apologize to his wife. She never deserved his anger.

Sounding more aggressive than he felt, he said, "Are you going to get on with it?"

But Drummond didn't speak. He stared at his hat and ran a finger over the lining. He appeared to be summoning the courage to tell his story, and that scared Max into a darker silence of his own.

At length, Drummond set his hat back on his head and stuck his hands inside his coat pockets. And he spoke. "I had been in the PI racket for a few years when this case came my way. Before that I was a beat cop — you remember that story?"

"Yeah. Dead woman's ghost kept crying out to you until you started believing."

He nodded. "Anyway, my old buddy from those days moved up the ranks quick. He became a detective — Detective Cooper — and whenever he stumbled into the weird cases of my world, I'd get a call. I never did find out how he got the department to pay for my services. Probably chalked it up to some kind of catch-all like *consultant* or *advisor*. We had fallen into a steady routine and all was good. Well, mostly good. I had just come off a hard case. Almost died — three times, actually — because of a ghost that didn't want to admit it was a ghost. So, like you, I was thinking no more.

"One night, I'm getting ready to close up the office, probably drink some whiskey and see if the pretty redhead waitressing at Mick's Bar wanted to spend a few hours together, when Detective Cooper stumbles through my door. He's drunk. I mean really soused. I helped him over to my couch, undid his shoes, and set a bucket nearby in case he had to throw up. Thought that was it. I'd lock up behind me and he could sleep it off. Figured he would tell me in the morning what heartbreak caused him to get blitzed. That was the typical reason Cooper drank heavy — a girl."

Max wanted to urge Drummond to get to the point, but he saw how each word popped out of the man like old stitches being cut. Each one hurt.

"Anyway, I'm getting ready to leave for the second time when Cooper sits bolt upright and looks straight at me. He said — and I'll never forget this — he said, 'You never told me this was real.' The way he said it, the horrified shiver in his voice, it reminded me of that first ghost I ever saw. How I stood there trying to comprehend what I was seeing, experiencing, and yet I was unable to get it through my head. That's how Cooper sounded. But the terror in his eyes told me that what he saw had to have been something far worse than a ghost floating around.

"It took him most of an hour to get it all out. Not a long story, but he had to stop many times in order to get hold of himself. What it came down to is that he got called in on a homicide case, and when he showed up at the residence, he saw a slaughterhouse. Two people murdered, a young couple — he said that their blood had been sprayed across every wall as if the murderer hacked off their limbs and twirled with the bloody parts high in the air. Worst of all, there was an empty bassinet. The murderer had taken the baby."

When Drummond paused longer than expected, Max asked, "What made him think it was a case for you?"

"While he processed the scene — made sure the proper photos were taken and all the evidence collected — he saw something that looked out of place. Just a piece of paper, really, but it was yellow and crinkled. He said it looked like parchment. On it, drawn in blood that he presumed to belong to the victims, he found a set of occult-like symbols. That's what he called them. *Occult-like symbols*. He even said that he felt a vibration in the air as he reached for the paper. At the time, he assumed it was a breeze from outside, but later he noticed that all the windows were closed.

"And then he picked up the paper.

"Two things happened to him at that moment — two things that made all that I did suddenly become real for him. First, a depressive sadness overwhelmed him. An unnatural weight of emotion took over and he dropped to his knees. Second thing, and by far the more convincing, he had a vision."

"A vision? For real?"

"Why would I make something like that up?"

"I didn't mean it like that. It just took me by surprise. I thought you had to have a gift like Sandra or at least be open to the supernatural for visions to work. But this wouldn't be the first thing about magic I got wrong. So, what did Cooper see?"

Drummond's head lowered and he took a shaking breath. "He saw children. Dead children. A dozen of them. All lined up shoulder-to-shoulder like fallen soldiers after a battle. I'll spare you the details, but Cooper shared with me every last one — down to the speck of blood on one child's frozen eye. And standing over all these bodies, he saw a woman. He knew right away she was a witch. Said that she had all the classic features — humpback, covered in a cloak, with a bulbous nose, and disgusting teeth. She even laughed like a witch."

After another silence, Max said, "That's a horrible story, but I don't see how that changes my mind. In fact, it's all the more reason to keep PB and J out of this kind of thing. I don't want them ending up like those kids."

"Let me finish," Drummond said, a harsh tone creeping into his voice. "I told you before that I had just come off a hard case, one in which I came close to dying more than once. I hadn't told anybody this, didn't even really admit it to myself, but when I thought no more, I had decided to hang it up. Not just no more magic cases, but no more entirely. Get out of this crazy business. Cooper's story only strengthened my resolve. I settled him back on the couch and went home, determined to never deal with the magic world again.

"But the next morning, Cooper called me from the station. That guy had amazing resilience, especially when dealing with a hangover. So, he calls me that morning to tell me that the witch had struck again. This time, she tore apart Mr. Robert Wellman — headmaster of the Greensboro Friends Home. It was a Quaker orphanage.

"Cooper was in a panic. He did a little digging and found that the couple with the baby were Quakers who served on the board at the orphanage. And now the headmaster was killed. Cooper knew his vision meant the orphans were in danger.

"And that was it. I wasn't about to let a dozen kids get ripped apart by some witch. Because if I did nothing, then nothing would be done. Cooper would have tried, but he didn't know the first thing about fighting witches and ghosts and such. Like it or not, I was the only one equipped to handle the case. That's true now about you and Sandra and me. We're the ones here to fight now. It's our job, and if we turn our back on it, innocent people die. Sometimes worse."

"I understand what you're trying to say —"

"Then understand this — once you started this, quitting never became a real option. People depend on you now, and I don't just mean Sandra, your mom, and the boys. I mean people who don't even know you yet. People who are going to find themselves faced with the world as it really is and they won't have anybody to turn to that they can trust."

"Except us."

"Exactly."

Max spun his chair toward the window looking at the backyard. Not much could be seen under the quarter-moon, but Max's eyes were not focused on the landscape anyway. His sight focused inward.

A lot of Drummond's words made sense, some even filled Max with a sense of pride — after all, the Hull family would still be out there ruining people as they saw fit if not for Max and his team. However, spells and curses existed long before he had been born. They would exist long after he died. Somebody always filled the role Max now had. If he stopped, somebody else would come along and protect people from the evil of the world.

But he couldn't guarantee that. Plus, it wasn't a matter of being replaced. It was a matter of numbers. Back when Drummond lived, he had met others who also fought witches and ghosts. Surely, there were others now. If Max closed The Porter Agency, those others would continue to fight, but they would be one agency down. One resourceful team less.

Max glanced at the door. *And what makes me think Sandra would let me close the agency?*

She would fight him, but deep down, he knew she would rather let it go than lose him over it. If he dug in and refused to budge, she'd let the agency die. So the real question came down to who was more important — those he loved or those who needed the agency's help?

He stood and tucked his shirt into his pants. Might as well get the argument over with — Sandra and Drummond were not going to take this well.

As he came around the desk, he glimpsed a shadow moving in the yard. Not wanting to spook whoever hid outside, Max continued to move toward the door. To Drummond, he said, "There's somebody outside."

"I'll check it out."

As Drummond passed through the window, Max entered the kitchen. He hurried by his concerned mother, slid into the garage, out the side door, and sprinted around back. Tearing around the corner, he saw the pale glow of Drummond by a line of trees bordering the backyard of their neighbors.

"He's here," Drummond said, waving a hand. "Gray suit and blue tie."

Max zeroed in on the man's position, but before he got too close, the man bolted across the yard. Max pursued while Drummond flew through the back corner of the house to get ahead of the man.

"You want me to freeze him?" Drummond asked. He could touch the corporeal world, but it caused him tremendous pain. His cold grip would certainly hurt the man, too, but as Max rushed down the side, he shook his head.

"Let him go," he said, halting at the edge of his property. The man vaulted over a small fence and weaved his way from one backyard to the next.

The bright beam of a flashlight played against Max's back, casting his shadow long upon the grass. He turned around to find Sandra and his mother standing in the doorway.

"Why'd we let him get away?" Drummond asked.

Staring back at the empty space where the man had been, Max set his jaw and fought back the urge to scream. Though strained, he managed to say in a calm voice, "There's no getting away, is there?" He looked to Drummond. "Even if I stop working the cases, even if I tell the whole world that I'm done with it all, they'll keep finding their way toward me. They'll keep threatening us, no matter what we do. Because they know that we know. And that means that we can jump back in at any point. Right? Once you know about magic, once you start getting involved, you can't get out."

"Sorry, pal. That's what I was trying to tell you. It's all part of the gig."

Sandra stepped closer. "What's going on?"

Putting his arm around his wife, Max swallowed hard and conjured his bravest face. "We're taking the case."

"I could've told you that." Sandra laughed. "In fact, I did."

Chapter 5

THE NEXT MORNING, Max waited in his downtown office for the others to arrive. He set out early, before sunrise, and stopped by the little bagel shop on the corner. A dozen bagels and several cups of coffee awaited his wife, his mother, and the boys. Not much of a peace offering, but enough to get them going on the right foot.

Kicking back in his chair, he looked upon the bookshelves that served as a home base for Drummond. Like the rest of the room, it had its function but lacked much of the charm of their original office. Of course, that office had come complete with an old curse, the Hull thumb pressing down on them, and a witch living down the hall.

Max smirked. "From the very start," he said. Witches, curses, power struggles — all of it had been with them from the first day they stepped foot in Winston-Salem. And from that same day, they had always persevered by plowing on straight through their troubles.

After taking such a brutal beating on their last case, Max could now admit that he had panicked. He had attempted to retreat, and that never worked. Even his masters in Tae Kwon Do could have told him that. They repeatedly taught that one must never turn his back on a threat. Always face the enemy.

Again, Max chuckled at himself. It amazed him that no matter how often he learned certain lessons, his mind still attempted to trick him into backing away. And yet, another aspect of martial arts followed the idea of knowing one's limitations and acting accordingly. As a newly-minted green belt, Max had some confidence, but he knew he couldn't pull of a flying jump back kick with any authority. Limitations mattered to survival.

Sandra and Drummond would argue that they were black belts when it came to the paranormal. Max wasn't so sure. But he did know that there was a serious threat to deal with, and for once, he had a sizable team to help him out.

The office door opened, saving him from his own spinning thoughts. The whole gang entered, and the bustle of people brought Drummond out of his bookshelf. The boys pounced on the bagels while Mrs. Porter and Sandra opted for the caffeine boost of warm coffee.

Over a mouthful of bagel, PB said, "I hear we got a new case."

"We do," Max said. "And I'm going to need everyone on this. I'm not sure how much we can trust the people who hired us, but they do need our help."

J sat on the floor next to PB and downed the last of one bagel as he reached for another. "Momma Porter said they paid up front. Can't be all that bad if they're paid up already."

Momma Porter? Max glanced at his mother but she shrugged it off. "Maybe. But somebody doesn't like them and is causing them trouble. We don't have much to go on regarding this mystery man."

"This the guy who spied on you last night?" PB asked.

"Yeah. Since we can't follow up on him yet, we're going to look into the Darden family. Try to find out *why* somebody is targeting them, and hopefully that will lead us to *who*."

Sandra nodded. "Sounds like a good approach. What do you want us to do?"

Despite all his misgivings, Max had to admit it felt good

to be organizing a case again. "Mom, PB, and Jammer J — I want the three of you to go to the Darden property. Don't let them know you're there. Don't even go through the gate. I want you to walk the entire perimeter of their land. It's a lot of land, so be ready for a hike. Anything you see that isn't fields, rock, trees, or animals, anything at all, you write it down. Also, mark the exact location of what you find."

He turned to Sandra. She smiled and said, "I know. You want me to check into the property history."

"You are the best at it. Also, I need you to swing by the Darden's lawyer and pick up a copy of Holly Darden's Will. While you all do that, I'll research the Darden family to see if I can find out who might have a reason to come after them. Any questions?"

Less than a minute later, they all left the office. All except Drummond. As Max booted up his laptop, he said, "Thanks for keeping quiet while my mother was here. She gets unsettled when I talk to you in front of her. Makes her think I'm going crazy."

"Watching you talk to empty air will do that. But I can't take credit for sensitivity or anything. I just didn't have anything to say."

"That doesn't always stop you."

"Hey, you try being a ghost for seven decades and see what happens. You'd rather I ended up like some of the ghosts we've seen — zombie-like and moaning and all lost in the head?"

Not wanting to indulge Drummond's fondness for argument, Max shifted to the task at hand. "You know what I want you to do."

"Yeah, yeah. I'll go to the Other and search for Aunt Holly's ghost." Drummond drifted back to his bookshelf. "You know, just because I'm the only one of us that can actually go to the Other, doesn't mean I can't do other things, too."

Max's mouth dropped as he faced Drummond. "Are you serious? I've agreed to take on the case, something I didn't want to do in the first place, and you're going to complain about how I handle it? And since when don't you get to do other things?"

Grumbling low, Drummond said, "Well, I didn't mean it literally. I just meant, aw, forget it."

The ghost disappeared, and Max wasted no time digging into the research. He would have preferred heading out to one of the libraries in Winston-Salem, the Z. Smith Reynolds Library at Wake Forest University being his favorite, but he did not expect to find much on the Darden family in books. He had not come across their name before which suggested that they were not a famous family in the community. Considering how far from the city they lived, he suspected they were rather reclusive and not the types that would warrant biographies or other non-fiction books written about them. Instead, he focused on census data — easily acquired online — and a few trusted sites that delved into local history.

After a few hours work, he grabbed lunch at Di Lisio's, a Mom-n-Pop Italian place Max had discovered recently. As he ate, it occurred to him that despite the Dardens staying out of the public eye, their name might still have popped up in a news article or two. He chided himself for not going that route right from the start. Where was his head in all this?

Hopping over to the Forsyth Public Library a couple blocks away, he searched through the old newspaper archives. By the time he finished and returned to the office, a clearer picture of the family had emerged. Mr. Mane's overview had been truthful, but it left out a lot. It wasn't pretty.

It started in Germany in the late-1800s. Witch hunts were common enough. People frightened of the strange and unexplainable created scapegoats wherever convenient. Max had little trouble believing that, on occasion, those living in a small farming town might stumble upon an actual witch. Whether on the run from pitchfork-wielding townsfolk or simply escaping before the town turned on them, the Dardens first showed up in New York City in 1792. Ezekiel Darden, his wife and four children were listed on a passenger manifest.

By 1793, Darden and family had moved to North Carolina. His name and family listing appeared again in tax records of North Carolina's Governor Tryon.

"Thank you, Governor," Max said to his laptop screen. Tryon kept meticulous records, most of which were preserved, digitized, and made available through online archives.

From those records, Max could see the Darden family's wealth grow. Ezekiel started with a small farm that struggled for two years which, according to Tryon's records, grew "an assortment of quality vegetables pleasing to both sight and taste." However, as the new century neared, Darden stopped growing vegetables for market and turned his meager fields over to the production of tobacco.

From that point on, the money rolled in. He bought the surrounding land (which reflected in greater taxes), and became quite successful. So much so that he needed more hands than he had with his family to maintain the fields. In 1802, Ezekiel Darden solved his problem by purchasing his first slave. He apparently had no distaste for it because he bought another three slaves before the month was out.

Max found little to point to the use of magic during this time; however, he also had difficulty finding reference to

Ezekiel's wife and children. In fact, an entire generation was barely mentioned. But by the 1840s, long after Ezekiel had passed away, the reality of the family practices began to show.

By that point in time, Daniel Darden had control of the plantation. The tobacco operation had grown significantly, encompassing over a hundred acres and employing twenty men. More significantly, they owned roughly forty slaves.

Daniel's wife, Charity, must have been feared by the slaves. Sales records showed that Daniel had to purchase house slaves nearly every quarter for three years. While the possibility existed that Charity was nothing more than a ridiculously demanding woman, Max suspected that her involvement in witchcraft leaned toward darker, blood magic. He couldn't prove it, though.

His cell phone rang — Sandra. Rubbing his eyes, Max pushed away from his laptop and stretched his legs. "Hey hon. What do you got?"

"Nothing much. I finished up on the property. Everything's in order. The only interesting part came right after the Civil War."

"I'm not surprised." That was the next key thing Max had learned. During the ramp up to the conflict, Daniel's two sons took opposite views towards slavery and the Confederacy. Abraham, the eldest, believed in his father's choices and volunteered to fight against the North should it be necessary. Luke, on the other hand, understood that times had changed, that what had once been acceptable could no longer continue, and most importantly, that they had been wrong. When the war finally broke out, Luke left the family and joined the Union.

After hearing this portion of the Darden history, Sandra said, "That lines up with what I found. After the war, Luke filed for ownership of the property. The Union army was looting like crazy, so Luke must have wanted to protect his family lands. Abraham died during the war, but the mother had a baby girl — Rebecca."

"Charity Darden would have been in her mid-forties at the time. Back then, that was seriously dangerous."

"If she was a witch, she could have cast a few spells to protect her. I can look into that later. What's interesting here is that Charity fought Luke for the land on behalf of Rebecca. She had Daniel's Will that gave her the property, and when she took Luke to court, she pointed out that he had betrayed them all by fighting for the Union."

"I didn't think women could own property back then. At least, not when a male family member had claim, too."

"Hence the fight. In the end, being male trumped betraying the South. They gave Luke the property."

Max hustled back to his desk and checked his notes. "Luke died in 1867."

"I guess it won't surprise you to learn that the court case finished out and granted him the property that same year."

"According to the obituary, he died while riding a horse that got frightened and threw him. Cracked his head open on a rock and bled out before he could find help."

"Want to wager that some witchcraft was behind the horse's behavior?"

"I don't take losing bets. Good work, hon."

"I'm off to the lawyer. See you soon."

Max stared at his laptop screen and clicked his tongue. The Dardens had done a remarkable job of staying out of sight. Other than Charity's obvious and deplorable abuse of her slaves and the story of Luke's fight for the family land, there was little more to go on.

They were a quiet family that kept to themselves and generally avoided any kind of gossip. Even during the Great Depression, they managed to garner little of the limelight.

Everybody knew they had a large tobacco farm, so it surprised nobody that they remained financially healthy during that period. After all, people continued to smoke — maybe more than before. Max found only one article, and it centered on Emily Darden donating money and volunteering her time at the soup kitchen.

All of this left Max with two distinct possibilities. Either the Dardens were a humble, quiet family that dabbled to one degree or another with magic but never truly amounted to much in that realm. Or the Darden women were powerful witches who had become masterminds at hiding their tracks. Yet if the latter were true, wouldn't he have heard about them during his time with the Hulls? Surely, the family that controlled magic usage in most of North Carolina and all of Winston-Salem would know about a powerful group of wealthy witches like the Dardens. Considering all the things the Hulls concerned themselves with and, in particular, the things they wrapped around Max's life, he found it hard to believe he would never once have heard of the Dardens.

"But that doesn't mean it can't be," he said, writing down these questions as they hit his mind.

Later in the day, his mother called. She and the boys had meandered around the property once and it took almost all day. They found nothing. And they were tired. She was taking them out for pizza and ice cream and would charge it to the agency.

"Sure, Mom. No problem."

"Why would it be a problem? We're working for you. The least you could do is feed us a little. Honestly, asking an old woman like me to walk acre after acre. You need to be more thoughtful of your employees."

Before she could really get going, Max told her to enjoy the dinner and that he had to get back to work. Drummond arrived twenty minutes later, but he also had nothing to show.

"I've got my contacts looking for old Aunt Holly, but so far, nobody's seen nothing."

"That's the operative word for today — nothing. Other than a dark history, and not that dark compared to most of our cases, we really don't have anything to indicate why this man is attacking them."

"Witchcraft — even if they never accomplished much with it — should be indication enough."

"Not enough to help us find who's behind this."

Max shut down his computer and planned to call it a night, when Sandra phoned again. "I've got the Will, and you're not going to believe this."

Before she spat out what she had learned, an idea popped in Max's head. "How far are you from the office?"

"Ten minutes."

"Great. Come pick me up. You can tell me all about the Will on the way."

"Where are we going?"

He grinned. "Back to the Dardens. I'm not going to waste another day on this case, if we can solve it all with a Will."

"But you haven't even heard what's in it."

"I know enough about this family, now. Trust me. Once they know that we know what's in the Will, the truth will come out. Chelsea Darden knows a lot more than she's letting on."

"Okay," Sandra said, and Max could hear the smile on her lips. "I'm on my way."

Max didn't know if what he said was true, but his instincts guided him in this direction. After all, the only contention in the family history surrounded a Will. And families, like history itself, tended to repeat.

Chapter 6

AS SANDRA DROVE SOUTHWARD, Max sat in the passenger seat with the harsh cabin light shining on the Last Will and Testament of Holly Charity Darden. Drummond floated in the back, reading over Max's shoulder.

"Wow," Max said when he finished.

Sandra said, "I know. It's hard to believe she would set things up like that."

"If I'm reading this right, Chelsea gets the house and all the land."

Drummond's cold arm reached over to point at the papers. "But it says she only gets the place provided that she never sells it and that she takes care of Beatrice Darden until Beatrice dies. I'm guessing that's Grandma Darden."

Sandra nodded. "That's right. But I asked Mr. Mane how any of that was enforceable, and he said many of these kinds of clauses aren't enforceable after a point. The house will go to her, but it's up to her sense of familial duty to not sell it."

"Considering how long the place has been in the family, I get the feeling she'll follow the rules."

"Don't forget," Max said, "the Dardens do have witches in their history. I'm thinking the kids may not be too keen on defying the will of ol' Auntie Holly, if there's even a remote chance the woman might come back."

Sandra chuckled. "True. The key thing, though, is that Chelsea doesn't get the money. All of the investments and cash holdings and such, all of it goes to Lane in the form of a trust fund managed by the Law Offices of Howard, Mane, and Jackson until she turns eighteen. Chelsea's going to need Lane for the money, and Lane will need Chelsea for the house — assuming Lane would want to stay on the family property."

"But the kicker is Alan."

"I know, that's what I really wanted you to see."

Max read it over once more to make sure he got it right. "According to this, Alan gets nothing. It's not just that he was excluded, there's a specific clause that states he is not to receive any of the property or its value, none of the cash or investments, absolutely nothing. I've heard of people being cut out of a will but never have I seen them written in specifically to write them out."

They pulled through the main gate and followed the winding path to the house. Max had called ahead. Normally, he would have showed up unannounced, not wanting to give them time to prepare for what he might ask, but the lateness of the hour and the fact that these people were paying for the Agency's services suggested a less surprising tactic.

"I hope it's okay, but we settled Grandma Darden in for the night," Chelsea said as she ushered Max and Sandra to a second living room. This one looked more like a hunting lodge — all wood with animal heads stuffed and mounted on the walls. Mostly deer heads but one lion and a full-upright bear in the corner. Next to a thin, closet door, Max noted an empty, glass gun rack.

"Who did all the hunting?" he asked.

"Aunt Holly's father. Chester. He loved all that kind of thing." Chelsea gestured to a couch that spanned one entire wall. "Please, make yourselves comfortable. Can I get you anything? Tea? Coffee?"

"No, thank you. It's late and we don't want to take up too much of your time. We've been working on your case, getting the background together."

She lowered to the edge of a chair nearby. "Oh, thank goodness. I honestly expected you to turn us away."

"You can thank my wife for that."

Drummond said, "Hey, you know it was me that turned you around."

Max offered a slight nod for Drummond's benefit. He didn't think Chelsea would want to know that a ghost had been hanging around with them, particularly one that influenced Max.

Sandra pushed things on track. "We're here tonight to interview you three siblings. We need to fill in a few gaps of the picture, and we're hoping to find some detail that will help us figure out who this man is that cast the spell on you."

"I can assure you," Chelsea said, "that we don't know who he is."

"But he certainly knows you."

She glanced into the hall. "I suppose I should call Lane and Alan down here."

"Just Alan," Max said. "We'd like to interview you all one-at-a-time. Makes it easier on us. Helps us keep track of things when all our notes are organized."

"Oh. Of course." She paused, fiddling with the hem of her skirt, and then with an abrupt motion, she stood. "I'll get Alan."

"Well," Drummond said after Chelsea left, "that wasn't weird."

A few minutes later, Alan entered carrying a beer by the neck. He wore pajama bottoms and a white T-shirt.

"You want to ask me some questions?" he said, plopping down into the chair Chelsea had occupied. Slouching down, he stretched his legs outward and balanced the beer bottle on his stomach.

Drummond circled the chair, making no effort to avoid passing through Alan's legs. "I've seen this type before. Acting like a slacker, like nothing matters, but trust me, it's all for show. Only people I've ever met who really felt the way this guy is pretending were drug addicts. And even they cared a lot about things — well, one thing — getting more drugs. Don't soft-peddle this guy. Go straight to the hard questions."

When it came to interview techniques, Max had learned to trust Drummond's advice. He saw no reason to stop now. "Alan, we wanted to talk with you about your Aunt Holly's Will."

"Yeah?" Alan shrugged. "Don't know much about it."

"I find that hard to believe. She wasn't very nice to you — leaving you nothing."

"I didn't expect anything from her. She never really liked me."

"Oh? Why didn't she like you?"

Drummond pointed at a twitching muscle near Alan's right eye. "See that? You're already getting to him."

Alan sat up and downed the remainder of his beer. After stifling a belch, he forced an unconvincing, nonchalant expression and said, "She was all big on the family lineage of witches and all that. I couldn't have cared less. I mean, I suppose it's interesting, but a bunch of superstition isn't really that important anymore."

With a slight edge in her tone, Sandra said, "You don't believe in magic? What about this spell that's keeping you in the house?"

He flicked his fingers like a bad actor portraying a wizard. "Magic spells? No. I don't know who has us locked down, and I don't know how he's doing it, but we are not the victims of a magic spell. Probably something like those invisible fences they use on dogs. I don't know. Physics was never a good subject for me. Whatever it is, I'm sure it's not magic."

Max said, "You're saying that Aunt Holly specified you were to get nothing because you refused to believe in witchcraft?"

"What can I say? She was a crazy bat."

"That's not a nice thing to say about the woman who took you in and raised you."

"Don't believe everything my sisters say about her. Aunt Holly could be nice and generous, but she had a mean streak, too. Especially for me."

"Because you didn't believe."

"Because witchcraft is a woman's business." Alan set his empty bottle on the floor and walked over toward the gun rack. He pressed a panel to the side and it popped open revealing a mini-fridge. Grabbing another beer, he said, "The lineage, the knowledge, all of the things that these witches practice passes from woman to woman. Sometimes a man comes along and gains the knowledge, but all of the real focus — the covens, the spells, the power — all of that is reserved for the women."

Sandra said, "But you don't believe in any of it. So, it doesn't really matter."

"Aunt Holly believed. That caused me enough trouble. But the Will? I don't care. When you grow up an orphan — even one that's got family taking you in — well, you learn to be a survivor. It doesn't matter to me what's in that Will because I'll end up just fine."

After they finished up with Alan, Max had Lane sent in. She sauntered in with teenage attitude oozing off her. Chewing gum and bopping her head to music on her phone.

Max pantomimed pulling out earbuds, yet she looked at him as if she had no idea what he meant. When she took the chair, she threw one leg over the armrest and made an exasperated show of turning off the music and removing her earbuds.

Drummond laughed. "Bet you're glad you chose not to have kids."

Before Max could speak, Sandra placed her hand on his knee and patted gently. She would handle this one. "Sorry to interrupt your evening."

Lane shrugged — a move she clearly picked up from her brother. "It's not like I can go anywhere."

"That's why we're here. We're trying to help fix this."

"So, why are you bothering with me? Chelsea said it was all some spell. Shouldn't you be trying to break it?"

"We are. But it'll help us if we can find the man that started this whole thing."

Lane rolled her eyes. "You don't need to find him. Just look into the books until you figure out which spell he used. If the anti-spell isn't there, I can show you how to cross-reference it all."

"You seem to know a lot about this."

"Aunt Holly raised me from when I was a baby. She taught me everything she knew about witchcraft."

"I guess you were her favorite."

"I suppose. She didn't like Alan. He fought with her about everything."

"And Chelsea?"

Another shrug. "Chelsea is a pleaser. Aunt Holly had no respect for pleasers. But she wasn't above using them either."

"Sounds like you and Aunt Holly were close. You must miss her a lot."

Lane buried her chin into her chest and eyed Max. Taking the hint, Max got up and walked over to a shelf of books on the wall opposite the gun rack. The titles ranged wide. Everything from hardcover classics like *The Red Badge of Courage, Dracula,* and *Crime and Punishment* to paperbacks by Stephen King and Lee Child. Nestled between *Dune* and *Catcher in the Rye*, Max noticed a thin, leather-bound book.

He pulled out the book and leafed through the pages. It was a journal filled with handwritten entries. A hand reached across his view and snatched the book.

"Nobody was ever allowed to look at that," Lane said, clutching the book to her chest.

"Was that Aunt Holly's?" Max asked.

"Of course. You think I'd care if you read Chelsea's journal?"

"The answer to your problems might be in there."

Lane jutted her head forward and said slowly, "Nobody is allowed to look at this. Get it?" She walked back to the chair and gathered her things. "This is Aunt Holly's private thoughts. We have to respect that. If she had wanted us to know what was in here, she would have made it clear in her Will."

Lane left with the journal, and Drummond pointed her way. "This family sure isn't big on subtlety."

As if answering his comment, the door opened and Chelsea entered. She must have been sitting in the hall during all the previous interviews. "Are you all done for the night?"

Max waved a hand toward the chair. "We still need to talk with you."

"Me? I can't imagine what else I could possibly tell you." She sat on the edge of the chair once more and placed her hands in her lap, forcing a calm and pleasant smile on her face.

"What can you tell us about this man who cast the spell? What did he look like? Did he say anything?"

"Oh, I don't recall that much detail. It all happened

rather fast, and it was so unexpected. Frankly, my head has been filled to the brim with a funeral and wedding plans. You'd think a wedding for me would be easy. I'm very organized and Enrique has gone with the opinion that whatever I want is fine. But that simply makes things so much harder. Every decision is mine now. You two are married, right?"

"Yes, we are."

"What was your wedding like? I'm eager for ideas."

Drummond said, "She's derailing the interview."

Max put out his hand to stop any further questions and to let Drummond know that he was fully aware of what had happened. "Please, Ms. Darden, you didn't hire us to discuss wedding plans."

"Well, I'm not being charged by the hour, so what's the harm?"

"We need to discuss your Aunt's Will. She left you the entire property but no money, and as we understand it, you can't sell the property either. Your sister, Lane, gets all the money, but it doesn't seem like she's going to be too generous. How are you going to maintain this estate, take care of your grandmother, pay property taxes, all of it — how?"

Chelsea smiled as she straightened her blouse. "Don't worry about me. Aunt Holly believed in that old Boy Scout motto — be prepared. She taught us that one well."

"You've got other money set aside for yourself?"

She snapped her fingers. "The hand. The man who did this to us wanted to get the Hand. I almost forgot about that."

"What is the hand?"

"Why, it's the only serious witchcraft related thing I've ever seen in this house. Come, I'll show you."

Chapter 7

CHELSEA LED THE WAY through carpeted halls with portraits lining the walls, up a flight of stairs with marble statuettes in recessed alcoves, and into a bedroom large enough to be a three-car garage. A canopied, four-poster bed dominated the lavish room. Heavy rugs and old oil portraits weighed down the decorations. An antique vanity overflowed with little glass bottles of crimson and emerald.

"This was Aunt Holly's room," Chelsea said as she entered a walk-in closet the size of Max's study.

The bed had a bearskin blanket and more pillows than one person could ever require. The air smelled of cinnamon. Most people would think the room ostentatious, but Max saw beyond that — after all, if one wanted to show off wealth, they did it in the living room, the kitchen, the foyer, and anywhere they expected guests to be. Certainly not the privacy of the bedroom. Bedrooms often reflected how a person truly saw themselves. Here, Max saw a woman who enjoyed her money and longed for a time that would not come back.

When Chelsea returned, she held a cardboard box. She placed the box on the bed and stepped back.

Max went over and opened the top. Inside, he found a glass cube. Inside the cube, he saw a petrified hand with a thick, green ring on the middle finger. The wrist had been cut clean and sewn tight. The fingers were long and bony, and the nails overgrown and chipped.

"It's a witch's hand," Chelsea said. "At least, that's what Aunt Holly always said. I never liked the thing. When she first brought it home, I was giving Lane a bath — she was still a toddler — and Aunt Holly came bursting into the house all full of cheer. She had always been big on restoring witchcraft to the family, particularly since my mother never showed any interest. I think the two fought a lot about it — about whether to teach me and Lane about it. That kind of thing. As it was, Aunt Holly never really told me much, and nothing about this hand. But that night when she came in all excited and showed off the hand, she said it would bring the family back to the path we were intended for. If that man hadn't mentioned it, I would've forgotten it was even here. I don't think Aunt Holly ever used it."

"What would you use it for?" Max asked.

"Magic, silly."

Sandra saved Max from snapping a sarcastic comment. "I'll look into it."

"Lane loved this thing," Chelsea went on. "When she was little, if I turned my back for a minute, she would take off through the house, and if given half-a-chance, I'd eventually find her here. Usually, she'd be in the closet staring at this hand. Frankly, I don't know why we bothered buying her any toys at all. This ridiculous thing entertained her for a long time. Until she got too old for such games."

Looking at Chelsea, Max said, "And the man, he wanted this?"

She nodded. "Maybe. I don't know. That night was such a blur."

Though he tried a few different angles, Max could not get anything else worthwhile from her. Sandra thanked the Dardens for their time and drove the way back to the office. The sun had set and they were tired, but when Sandra parked the car, Max bounded up the stairs, shoved open the door, and slid right into his chair.

As he powered up his laptop, Drummond glided

through the office walls. "That was a great haul. You got a lot of useful information."

"Maybe. We certainly got a good picture of the family dynamics."

"That's what I'm talking about. Don't discount that. In all my time as a detective, I'm telling you, understanding the relationships of the suspects often leads to solving the case."

Sandra walked over to Max, bent down, and kissed his cheek. "I see that look in your eye."

"What look?"

"The one that says you plan to be here all night doing research."

With a bashful grin, Max said, "Oh, that look. The way I figure it, the faster we get through all of this, the faster I'll be done with the Dardens. And I'll tell you flat out, I don't like them."

"I get the feeling they don't like us that much, either."

"Yeah, and they haven't even met Drummond."

From the bookshelf, Drummond said, "Watch it, pal, or you'll be on your own tonight."

Max laughed. "Quick, honey, give me some good insults to throw. I could use a quiet night alone."

"Very funny, but I think you'll want to hear what I got to say about that petrified hand."

"Oh?"

"It reminds of a petrified man I once saw — the Spaghetti Man."

Sandra kissed Max again. "There's that look. I think I'll go home, check on your mom, and get some sleep. At least one of us should be functional tomorrow morning."

After she left, Max spun his chair toward Drummond. "Okay, out with it. What's the Spaghetti Man?"

Drummond's eyes sparkled as he swept in closer. He

tipped back his hat like a cub reporter who had landed his first big scoop. "I haven't thought about Spaghetti Man in ages, but yeah, the more I picture him, the more I think he and that hand looked a lot alike."

"Okay, then who is he? What's the story?"

"I wasn't even born when it happened, but back in 1910, maybe 1911, a traveling carnival came through the town of Laurinburg. It's a little place in the southern edge of the state. The story was that this guy — hold on, let me think ... he's name was Cancetto Farmica."

"You still remember the guy's name?"

"How are you gonna forget a name like that? Besides, this is a famous little story around here. Everybody knew about it back then. One of those things you tell over and over."

"So, this is more tall tale than a real story."

Drummond's brow lowered. "Not at all. This is how it went down. And if you shut up long enough, you'll see why I can stand by the veracity of this story."

Max motioned locking his mouth and tossing the key.

"Okay, then," Drummond said. "Now, Cancetto is working on the carnival and gets himself killed in a fight. Don't know what it was about, but the man who killed him used a tent stake. Cancetto's father hears about it and travels to Laurinburg to take his son's body to the McDougald Funeral Home. He gives a whole tearful song about his son and how meager their finances are. In the end, the McDougalds agree to ten dollars down for their services and the rest on a payment plan. Cancetto's father agrees and promises when he returns, he will have more money and instructions for how he wanted the burial done.

"And that was it. Nobody at the funeral home ever heard from Cancetto's father again.

"But Mr. McDougald held good faith in people. He

figured someday the father, or some other relative, would return. So, he saved the body. He popped it in a box and stood it upright in the garage. Since the locals didn't really know Italian names, and many probably didn't even know the guy's name, they simply called him Spaghetti. Probably not an acceptable thing anymore."

"Definitely not."

"Back then, people weren't so overly-sensitive."

"We're not overly-sensitive. We just realize that we are not the only — oh, forget it. I'm not going to change you. Get on with your story."

"It could've stopped there, but then I would never have known about it. By the time I was thirteen, I knew plenty. Spaghetti had become a bit of a tourist attraction. People came from all over the country to see this guy. When I was little, kids would dare each other to go check out the box with the body in it. Of course, we all boasted we'd do it, but few of us ever had a real chance. During the Depression, your folks weren't going to agree to drive all the way to Laurinburg just so you can prove yourself by peeking at a corpse.

"Except I actually got to go. My mother had her mental issues, and every now and then she'd get it in her head to take me someplace strange without telling anybody. Usually it was a cavern or a two-bit freak show or something like that. I figured if I told her about Spaghetti, she might be intrigued enough to take me to see it. I was right. So, I did see the body, and the skin on that thing looked a lot like that witch's hand."

Max said, "But this guy was embalmed. Unless you think the McDougalds used magic."

"No, not magic. But then, we have no reason to think that the witch's hand was preserved using magic. We don't even know if, in fact, the hand belonged to a witch."

"That's right."

"And listen to this — Spaghetti continued to draw crowds all the way until 1972. Sixty years. Would've probably gone longer but this congressman from New York — Biaggi — he heard about our Italian attraction and yelled and hollered about it being disgraceful and a slap in the face of all Italians. That kind of thing. He stirred up enough people that eventually the funeral home buried Spaghetti in Hillside Cemetery. And one of the snazzy things about being a ghost — I remember this happening. I remember hearing all about Biaggi. I also recall a rumor that Cancetto's body was buried under several feet of concrete just in case somebody came along with the idea of digging him back up.

"That's it. That's as much as I remember of the story."

Max rested his chin on his hand as he thought. "It's a great story, but I'm not seeing the connection. I mean, obviously, Spaghetti Man was embalmed and, in a sense, petrified. So was the hand. But I suspect we could find thousands of well-preserved corpses all over the state."

"Not like this. That hand and Cancetto's body had the same general color and, for lack of a better word — I swear, don't you ever mention that I said this — but they share a vibe."

Max's arm slipped off the chair as he laughed. "A vibe?"

"Hey, I heard some people use it in the sixties. Maybe the seventies. The point is that both of them had a feel about them. I mean the second I saw that hand, I felt like I was a kid staring at Spaghetti. That can't be coincidence, and you know exactly why."

"Because there are no coincidences."

"That's right. Now, do me a favor, and look into a possible connection here. I know it's a long shot, but I'm telling you, I got a gut feeling about this."

"Don't you mean *a vibe?*"

Drummond brought his hat down and shook his head. "I knew I shouldn't have said anything."

Chapter 8

USUALLY, WHEN MAX FOLLOWED a line of research that looked promising, he felt a spark inside, a flash of excitement that told him he should keep pushing in that direction. Drummond's Spaghetti Man story lacked that spark. Unfortunately, Max had no other inspiration to follow.

When you got nothing, any lead is a good lead. One of Drummond's teachings that Max took to heart. He rested his fingers on the keyboard and got to work.

After about two minutes of staring at an empty search bar, Max leaned back in his chair. It was tough focusing when a ghost hovered overhead. Drummond clapped his hands once and Max yelped as he bounced in his chair. "Thanks for looking into this, pal. While you do that, I'm going back in the Other and find out if any of my informants got anything for me. I'll see you in the morning."

Trying not to scream about his pounding heart, Max gritted his teeth. "Okay. Do whatever you're going to do. I'll be here all night."

"I may have another stop or two besides those strictly related to the case."

Max raised an eyebrow. He stopped himself from clarifying that his *do whatever* comment had not been an accusation, and instead used another teaching from Drummond — when a suspect volunteers information, even under a false presumption, best to keep quiet and let them talk.

"She's not my girl, exactly," Drummond said. "She's just a gal from the 1800s who has an appreciation for 20th century men. Said she likes my hat."

Max winked and turned back to his computer.

"Oh, shut up," Drummond said and disappeared.

While chuckling to himself, Max's research brain kicked in. He started with a Google search on Spaghetti Man. Right at the top of the results, he found a CBS News puff piece outlining the general story that Drummond had told. He had no expectation that deeper digging would go as easily.

One search led to another. One article linked to a different article. Crawling through discussion boards, following link after link, pulling up archived records, and skimming through pages upon pages of old newspapers, Max struggled to find anything linking the witch's hand to Spaghetti.

But he did find some initials that kept reappearing — E.W. The letters where written in a rounded script and could be found on plenty of paperwork related to the funeral home. But nowhere could Max find a name that matched those initials.

At some point after three, Max recalled resting his head back. He closed his eyes. Just for a second. He promised. Just a second and then back to work.

"Rise and shine," his mother said.

Max jolted hard, his knee slamming into the underside of his desk.

"Oh, sorry, dear. I didn't mean to startle you." Mrs. Porter had a dust cloth in her hand and a pot of coffee gurgling from the sideboard near the bathroom door. "Have you been here all night?"

Waking up his computer, Max checked the time — 8:27 am. His mother walked over to the windows and opened the blinds. Bright morning light streaked into the office.

"You should be more careful about your work habits," she went on. "It's one thing to work all night through when you're in your twenties, but you're older now. The body slows down and can't snap back like it once did. You've got to respect that or your body will make you regret it." She grabbed an empty mug next to the coffee machine and took it to the bathroom sink. "Do you remember Ronald Lewis? Oh, you probably were too young to remember him. He used to come by the house every month or so with a basket of goodies — mostly food but always a toy or two for you. I'm pretty sure he thought he was charming me, but I had no interest. Especially because he didn't look after himself. Always working hard, talking about driving twelve hours here or seventeen hours there. Whatever it took to get to a potential sale — oh, he was in sales for some assembly line company or something. I don't know. I never paid too close attention. But that's not the point. The point is he pushed too hard, and one day, you know what happened?"

She paused, and though Max knew she wanted him to ask, he still needed his morning coffee before he felt like talking. Instead, he borrowed a page from the Dardens — he shrugged.

"Well, I tell you," Mrs. Porter said, returning with the mug, filling it with steaming coffee, and handing it over to her grateful son. "Ronald Lewis got older and his body said *No more*. He drove that car so hard, a tire blew out, he lost control and drove right off the side. Flipped the car three or four times and he died before help could arrive."

Max paused mid-sip. "What? His car tire blew out? What does that have to do with taking care of your body?"

"If he had gotten proper rest, he would have been more thoughtful about making sure his car was in good working order." She pulled out a bottle of cleaner from under the sink and squirted it on the bathroom mirror.

Max continued to drink his coffee until half was gone. Only then did his brain start to function properly again. He moved a few papers around, organizing his notes, but he kept seeing his mother cleaning the office, and he had to stop.

"You don't have to do that," he said.

"Do what?"

"Clean. You're not the maid in this outfit."

She moved from wiping the mirror to the sink. "I don't mind. Gives me something to do."

Max walked over to the bathroom and sipped more of his coffee. "You sure? I mean, about all of this. Being here. You left all your friends and your home and everything."

"I didn't have many friends anymore, and I gained more than I lost. I'm here with you. Plus, those boys are delightful."

He watched her clean, unsure how to say what he thought without offending her. "Well, if you change your mind, I mean if you regret your decision, I'd understand."

"Are you trying to get rid of me?" She said it playfully, but Max knew all of his mother's tones. A sharp bite snapped beneath the surface of her voice.

"Not at all." He returned to his desk, thumbing the paper with E.W. jotted at the top. "I just don't want you to feel like you made a mistake. You spend all your time here at the office or with the boys, and I don't see you getting to know anybody else."

"You mean anybody my own age?"

With a guilty grimace, he said, "Don't you want to talk with somebody who knows the same things you do? Lived through the same things?"

His mother crossed the office to wrap her arms around him. "Oh, Max. That's sweet of you to worry, but I'm fine.

I've only been here a few months. You got to give these things time. I'll meet some of my peers, don't fret." Breaking from the embrace, she whisked on her coat. "I'm going to that lovely little bagel shop on the corner. You need some breakfast."

As the office door closed, Drummond appeared. "What was that all about? You trying to get rid of her?"

"No." Max tapped his chin as he stared at the door. He hadn't meant to imply he wanted her to leave. Rather, he wondered how long she would stay. Her talk of taking care of the body and the fact that most of the people she knew back home were dead had forced Max to consider his mother's mortality.

Then why was I making it sound like I wanted her gone?

Articulating his feelings in this matter proved harder than he had expected. Especially considering that he only intended to articulate them for himself.

Drummond snapped his fingers in front of Max's face. "Wake up, there. We got work to do."

"Right." Max rapped his knuckles on his desk. "So, I checked deep into everything I could find on Spaghetti Man, and I came up with a lead for us. It's not much, but it's something — the initials E.W."

"Edith Walker."

Max's skin prickled. "What?"

"That's her name. Edith Walker."

"I've been at this all night and you already knew?"

"You need more coffee. Look, foggy brain, I spent a lot of the night working, too."

"I thought you were playing time-traveling lover with Miss 1800s."

"I wasn't going to be with her all night. Especially since we're ghosts. We don't sleep, and there's only so much cuddling a guy can take. Now, you want to know more details of my love life or you want to hear about Edith Walker?"

Max drained the last of his mug and set it on the table. "Edith Walker. Please. And for the record, I never want to know details of your love life."

A sly grin crossed Drummond's face. "Fine. But you're missing the better story. Anyway, I met with my informants — no news on Aunt Holly — but I got to thinking. A guy like Cancetto, dying so violently and with all that had happened to his body, well, there was a good chance he'd be in the Other, too. So I went looking."

"You found him?"

"No. But after talking with a few sources, I did have a nice sit-down with a lady from 1927 who had the exact same look as Cancetto and the hand. She told me that we're looking in the wrong place. The funeral home had an off-the-books employee — Edith Walker. She, apparently, worked as an embalmer for the unusual cases."

That got Max's full attention. "Are you saying she handled witches and such that died?"

"That's right. And when I say she was *off-the-books*, I mean it in spades. The McDougalds never even knew. She had stolen the funeral home key, made a copy, and she would sneak in at night to take whatever she needed. She also used their paperwork to requisition supplies as she needed."

"How could the McDougalds not know? They'd see the papers."

"Because the witches knew, too. And they cast spells for the McDougalds to forget about anything related to Edith Walker."

"Including the papers. But why did the witches help her? She wasn't one of them."

"Sometimes, no matter how much of a witch's life you

lived, when your number comes up, you get a whole lot more into traditional burial matters. If you wanted that, then instead of a pagan burial, you went to Edith Walker."

"You think this woman is still alive? She'd be at least a hundred and ten years old."

"She'd also be a woman with a lot of witches as friends."

Max thought back to an early case in which they met a man under a curse that had kept him alive for over two hundred years. He had also seen magic used to reduce the aging process. He had to keep reminding himself that when it came to age, magic broke the rules.

"Okay. Your source for this information is —"

"The ghost of one of her clients."

"That source wouldn't happen to know anything about a petrified hand, maybe?"

Drummond adjusted his coat and lifted his chin. "What kind of detective do you think I am?"

"A good one. So, what did your source say?"

"Doesn't know anything about it. Nobody I asked knew anything about the hand."

Max wanted to grab his coat and rush out the door. He could tell Drummond felt the same way. "It's a bit early to go barging in on the lady. Plus, my mother is getting bagels." He waved his hand to stop Drummond's inevitable comment. "Let me have some breakfast with her, make sure she's doing okay, give her a little time with her son, that kind of thing. Then I'll look up Edith Walker's address and we can go pay her a visit. Okay?"

"Fine, fine. But what am I supposed to do in the meantime?"

Thankfully, Mrs. Porter opened the office door, saving Max from having to suggest entertainment options to a ghost. The bagel and coffee breakfast went down like a lump — mostly because Max's mind swirled around Edith

Walker and her potential to help the case. He tried to focus on his mother, but by the end, she patted his hand and said, "Go work on your research. I'll finish cleaning."

Max offered a sheepish smile before dashing back to his computer. He found the address with ease, grabbed his coat and car keys, and headed out. By the time he started the car and buckled his seatbelt, Drummond had appeared in the passenger seat.

"You're not going to want to come," Max said.

"What are you talking about? Of course, I want to."

"Edith Walker is in her nineties and —."

"So? I can handle old people just fine."

"Yes, but she's dying. She lives in hospice care."

Drummond paused. "Oh."

For both Drummond and Sandra, hospitals were difficult places to be since they both could see all the ghosts. In a hospital, there were many. But in a hospice, ghosts overwhelmed the place.

"Maybe I'll sit this one out," Drummond said.

"Good idea. I'll let you know what I find out as soon as I can."

As Max drove off, Drummond disappeared.

Chapter 9

MAX DROVE AROUND THE BLOCK TWICE, then pulled over to check the address on his phone. Odd. He had it all down correct, yet he found himself in a suburban neighborhood. The address itself led to a two-story, tan house at the end of a cul-de-sac. No sign outside. Nothing to indicate a medical facility.

He parked on the street in front of the mailbox and took the brick walkway to the front door. After ringing the bell, which played the alien five-note sequence from *Close Encounters of the Third Kind*, Max considered driving back to the office and delving into his research again. This couldn't be the right place.

But the front door opened, and a large woman wearing Winnie the Pooh nursing scrubs looked at him. She had a charming smile and spoke with such a caring tone that Max's view of a hospice instantly changed.

"Is this Garden Hospice?"

"Why yes it is. Welcome. I'm Lee. Come on in."

Max entered the converted house and wrinkled his nose — a stale, sickly odor permeated the air.

Lee said, "Are you here visiting or do you need a room for someone?"

He wanted to ask how the heck they managed to operate this place. This couldn't be legal, yet Lee showed no alarm at a stranger knowing about it. In fact, the open secrecy of the place reminded him of the way witches lived.

Max's gut clenched. His eyes searched the room, picking out the small details — the assorted colored candles on a shelf, the woman asleep in a chair with a book that looked older than her, the man in a wheelchair with an IV of an oddly-dark liquid, the woman with a cane that appeared to be made of bone. Could this really be a hospice for those who knew about magic?

"Sir? Are you okay?" Lee touched his arm but snatched it back as if she had received an electric shock. "Oh, I'm sorry. Are you here for yourself?"

"Excuse me?"

"Obviously, your curse isn't debilitating yet, but if you're here to set up a room for future use, I'm afraid Shelly's not here today. She's our long-term sales person. Handles all the bookings for those expecting to need us in a year or two."

Max's hand rubbed the spot on his chest where he had been cursed. He spent plenty of time trying not to think about it and plenty more thinking about it, but he always ended back at the same point — nothing he could do. Not yet. Not until they found a witch they could trust who also had enough strength to break the curse. Or, perhaps, not until Sandra became that witch — something that sent Max's thoughts spiraling down if he let them.

"No," he managed. "Not for me. I'm visiting. Edith Walker? Is she still here?"

Lee's face lit up. "You know Edith! Oh, she's going to be delighted. I don't think she's had a visitor in over a year. And that's a shame when you consider that most people here don't stay that long."

"May I see her?"

"Of course. Come, come. Follow me."

She led the way up to the second floor and down the hall. The four bedrooms of the house had been divided into eight smaller rooms. It would be a tight fit, but most of the residents did not appear to mind. Nor did anybody have much in the way of possessions to fill up the rooms. At least, not that Max could see.

One room on the right was empty, and Max's mind flashed an image of his mother in that bed. His chest tightened. Before he could consider how he might feel sitting next to that bed, holding her hand, listening to her labored breaths, Lee stopped and opened another door.

"Edith?" she said. "You awake?"

Max entered the tiny enclosure. Though the room smelled of stale sweat, the meager furnishings had been kept clean. A knit blanket — black with a gold pentagram — had been spread on the bed. In the doorway, Max spied a set of arcane symbols drawn with an unsteady hand. Edith Walker sat in a wheelchair facing half-a-window. Presumably, the other half shed light on her neighbor's room.

Lee pulled a blanket from a narrow hall closet and placed it on Edith. "You have a visitor. Take a look." To Max, she added, "You can sit on the bed."

Max complied, but Edith did not move. After tucking the blanket in at the sides, Lee turned the wheelchair to face the bed. Her hands jumped off the chair as if she had been shocked. Forcing a laugh and giving Edith a stern look, Lee said, "Don't be naughty." She flashed another delightful smile at Max, waved goodbye, and left the room.

At first, Max thought it strange that they let him in without any proof that he actually knew Edith Walker. But then it dawned on him that this hospice was filled with witches and other magic-using folk. Nobody had to worry here. At least, not from mundane things like thieves.

"Ms. Walker?" Max said.

No response.

"I'm Max Porter. I was hoping you could talk with me a little about the funeral home you lived next to back in 1927 or so."

No response. Not even a flicker of light behind her eyes.

"Ms. Walker, do you remember the Spaghetti Man?"

Her head lifted slightly. With quivering lips and an equally quivering voice, she said, "Charlie took me to the drugstore. Got me a brown cow. It was so good, I wanted another, but I only had two-cents and you know what Mr. Holstein did? He waited until the counter was empty and he gave me a second one for two-cents. He winked at me and said that for a special girl like me, he'd lower the price."

"Did Charlie help you at the funeral home?"

"Not at all, silly beans. Charlie wouldn't want anything to do with that. Shucks, he never even believed me when I told him I'd met a witch."

Trying not to sound too eager, Max said, "You met a witch? Tell me about that."

But Edith's glazed attention drifted toward the window. She stopped speaking.

"Edith? Can you tell me about Charlie?"

No response.

Max remained on the bed, straining for some secret word that might open her mind. But she sat empty and limp like a ragdoll. He waved his hand in front of her face but got no reaction.

"Sorry to bother you," he said on his way out.

Lee blocked his way in the hall. "Leaving already? You have to give her more time. She has her lucid moments, but they're not consistent. You have to wait around for them."

"Unfortunately, I can't spend the whole day here. At least, not today."

"Then you'll come back? It's good for someone like Edith to have anybody she can look forward to seeing. Even somebody who isn't family or a friend."

Max's guilty blush answered her accusation. "I never

said I was anything but a visitor."

"I know." She led the way back to the front door. "Trust me on this, I never once feared for Edith. If you were here to cause trouble, you would never have made it to the stairs."

"I don't doubt it."

"What exactly are you here for? Edith never really did anything bad and she never did anything that got her noticed either."

"I'm a detective, of sorts, and I'm looking into an incident that tied Edith with an old story called the Spaghetti Man."

"I see. Her funeral home days."

"You know about that?"

Lee waved her hand as if showcasing the entire room. "I know everything about each one of my patients. It's part of the job."

"Then maybe you can help me. I'm trying to find out—"

She giggled. "Oh, bless your heart. You really think I'm going to share personal information of my patients with you? Dear, let me make this clear. You are welcome to come visit Edith anytime you want. You are welcome to ask her questions and listen to her answers — if she gives any. And anything she wants to share with you is her business to share. But I will not betray the confidence of these wonderful people. You understand?"

"Of course. I'm sorry."

"No need to be sorry. Now go on about your day, and I look forward to seeing you back here again soon."

When the door closed behind him, Max stood on the porch for a few seconds. Whenever he thought he had a basic grasp of the world around him, something new jarred his reality. First, he met Drummond — an actual ghost. Then he learned of witches and curses. And ever since, he seemed to stumble into one darker region after another. Here he learned that there existed a greater level of infrastructure to the witching world than he realized — a woman who handled burial matters and a hospice that catered toward the magically inclined.

This was the kind of thing he had wanted to escape when he turned down the case. Yet, as Drummond had made clear, this was the kind of thing he needed to learn about. Too often, a world as complex and complete as this would smack into the world the majority thought of as reality. Somebody had to be there to keep the peace, ease the understanding, and if necessary, fight back.

He walked back to his car, lost in his thoughts. He never heard the man approach, never knew he was in danger. That all changed when the man grabbed him by the shoulders and shoved him into the car door.

Chapter 10

MAX BOUNCED AGAINST THE CAR, his chin colliding with the window. A strike landed on his hip and another in the back. He expected a third hit, perhaps in the leg, but none came. He turned around to face his attacker — the man that had cursed the Dardens and spied on his house.

Like before, the man wore a gray suit with a blue tie. But he also covered his hands in gray driving gloves, his head in a gray bowler, and his face with a blue scarf. He hid every easily recognizable feature except his eyes, and those were a common brown.

His punches, though forceful, had been clumsy. He had hit Max's side when he could have aimed higher to strike the kidneys or even higher to break a rib. His follow up had been in the back — a strong, well-protected part of the body. And then, while he still had Max surprised, he could have struck the head or swept a leg. Instead, the man backed off, letting Max turn around.

Setting his feet in the stance he used for sparring, Max raised his fists. This man could wield magic, but he did not appear to know how to fight.

"You got something to say?" Max asked. "Or did you simply want to hit me?"

The man lunged forward with a punch. Max's left arm dropped in an arc, blocking the punch away. Another lunge from the man, and again Max blocked the punch with a side motion of his arm.

"This is stupid," Max said. "You obviously followed me here. You want to warn me away? Is that it? You want to tell me to back off the case? Go ahead. Consider me warned. We don't have to do this."

The man jumped at him, but Max's feet slid to the side, evading the attack while keeping good balance. He pivoted to stay facing the man.

"Come on. Stop it. You delivered your message. We don't need to —"

A flurry of punches soared at Max. His arms moved from one to the next, blocking and deflecting all but two. He took a hit to the shoulder, which barely registered, and a stronger punch landed in his gut. That one he felt.

But he didn't double over and he didn't lose his breath. He simply leaped back to create a safe distance, reset in his stance, and took a moment to check himself. His heart pounded — not from fear or fighting but from excitement that his martial arts training actually had worked. In that second of thought, however, he had lost focus. The man's fist flew upward and popped Max in the chin.

He stumbled back against the car, and the man followed up with a punishing blow to his stomach. This time, Max did fall over. A knee smashed Max's head against the car. His vision swam as he felt his body roll onto the pavement.

The man crouched over Max. He smelled of wood polish. In a husky voice, he said, "Now, you've been warned. Stop helping the Dardens or I'll use my magic on you, too."

He stood, kicked Max in the thigh, and walked away.

Max held his stomach and watched the man leave. He stayed still, not wanting to alert the man, and saw the man climb into a blue BMW. Though clumsy enough to get into his car in front of Max, the man had parked far enough away that Max failed to get a plate number.

Groaning, Max climbed to his feet. He rubbed his jaw and tasted blood on his tongue. Not bad for a new blue belt. He guessed that in a year or so he would earn his black belt and might even remember to throw an effective punch back instead of blocking the whole time.

He glanced at the hospice house. Nobody appeared to notice him. Either that, or all eyes that had watched the fight conveniently discovered something else to look at when Max turned his attention their way.

He thought about going back into the hospice and questioning Lee or anybody else lucid enough to have witnessed the fight. The witches of North Carolina were a tight group. They all knew each other or, at least, knew of each other. Surely, one of them would have heard about this man.

But they were a tight-lipped bunch, too. At least, they were tight-lipped until they discovered an angle in which talking benefited them. Nobody would give him anything useful. In fact, his last hope for a lead had been Edith Walker.

He got in his car, called Sandra, and asked her to meet him in the office. "I need to be patched up a little."

"On my way. What happened?"

"I'll tell you later. It's not like we have anything else to do. This case has reached a final dead end. We're done."

Chapter 11

MAX WINCED AS SANDRA patted rubbing alcohol on his chin. He sat on the toilet in the office bathroom as she knelt before him.

"Quit being a baby," she said. "You've had worse than this."

"Doesn't take the sting out, though."

She pressed a Band-Aid on, using more pressure than required, and put away the first aid kit with harsh motions.

"What's wrong?" he asked.

"You. Wanting to drop the case because things got hard. I shouldn't be surprised. You made it clear you didn't want this case in the first place."

She stomped off to her desk. Max followed. "It's not like that," he said. "You know me better. I said we'd take the case, and I meant it. But we have nothing left to go on."

"We've got this man. We've got Edith Walker."

"Other than driving a blue BMW, we've got nothing to help us locate this man. Our only real lead was Edith Walker, and she's not clear in the head. I could talk to her until the day she dies and I'll never get anything. Even if what she said was good information, I'll never know it."

"What about the name she mentioned? Charlie?"

"Great. Charlie who? Walker? According to what I found, her husband was Desmond Walker. They never had any kids and Desmond died ten years ago."

"Maybe Charlie is her brother."

"I checked. Edith's maiden name is Hobb. She had no siblings. Charlie could have been a friend, a neighbor, her first lover, anything. But without more information, we'll never know. And from what she said about him, I don't think he matters to this case."

Sandra pounded her fist against her desk. "But look at where you found her. A hospice for witches? You know she has something worthwhile locked in her head."

"What good is it when we can't get to it?"

She reached for her keyboard. "What if I can give you something to change that?"

"Honey, let it go. You don't need to be using witchcraft for this. You don't really need it at all."

"Don't do that."

"What now?"

"Don't talk to me like I'm a junkie. We both have skills to use, and I'm going to use mine." Her fingers clacked away. "You should be more worried about our other partner."

Max looked to the bookshelf. "What's the matter with Drummond?"

"If I knew that, I'd be telling you directly. But something is definitely wrong. He's been a bit edgy lately, ever since we started this case. And he can't sit still."

"He never sits still."

"Not like this. He's acting like he has to have something to do — like a distraction. Anything to keep his mind from thinking about whatever is bothering him."

"I hadn't noticed."

Sandra paused to read something from a website. "He doesn't like for you to see him vulnerable. So, he acts tougher around you. But you've been off chasing down leads while I've been here working. I've had to come up with things for him to do like he's a little kid or something." She stopped typing and stared straight at Max. "And I had to do it all while your mother cleaned the office for the millionth time. She had the nerve to compare her constant cleaning to our lack of cleaning in the house."

Max backed away from the desk. "I know. I'm sorry. It's only a few weeks more until her apartment is available."

"She better watch it or I'll try out some new spells on her."

Max started to speak, but Sandra shushed him. She sat closer to her computer as she read. "This might work. I need to check a few books, but this might do it."

"Care to explain?"

"You know about wards and curses. Well, there are also charms."

"We've come across a charm or two before."

"Not like this. We can take an object — usually a crystal pendant — and put a spell into it so that it releases later."

"You mean like a delayed spell? A time release?"

"That's right. I should be able to take a stone and put a spell into it that will help Edith Walker remember. It'll wake her up for a few minutes and let her tell you what you need to know."

Max walked back to the bathroom to check his bruised face in the mirror. "I'm not trying to pick a fight here, but are you sure? I mean, if that was possible, if you could put a spell in a necklace to use at will later, why wouldn't all the witches we know be doing that?"

"Well, it's not exactly stable."

He glanced out at her. "Is it going to explode?"

Copying book titles off her screen, she said, "It's minor magic, first off. And if it fails, the stone might shatter, making it useless to use again. Also, it's hard to regulate the strength of the spell's release. So, it's not very reliable. That's why most charms are for things like good luck or mood alterers — like a love inducer. If you want something seriously done, you need to sit down in a circle and cast a true spell. But from what you told me, nobody in that hospice is going to allow someone like me to come in and start casting spells."

"Probably not."

She stopped and looked straight at him. "Here's the deal. I'll make a charm. You take it to Edith and give it a try. If it works, great. We go from there. If it fails, then we tell the Dardens we're off the case. But first, we've got to know that we tried everything."

He wanted her to know that he really meant to stay on the case and that most of his complaints were out of frustration. Even if the charm failed, he wouldn't hold her to giving up on the Dardens. Not only because of what Drummond had said, but because he had seen how much this meant to her.

But he suspected she understood all of that. She was his wife. She knew him. All he had to do was simply nod and say, "Sounds good."

Her smile confirmed it all. As she rushed off to make her charm, Max got a bite to eat. Before the day was out, he knew he would be back at that hospice. Considering the attack from the man and the possibilities of what Edith Walker might say, Max thought he would have to be ready for anything.

Chapter 12

MAX PARKED IN FRONT OF THE HOSPICE. In his coat pocket, he carried the charm Sandra had made. Though nothing more than an almandine garnet wrapped with coarse twine, it tugged on his coat as if it had been set with a lead weight. According to crystal lore, the garnet held properties of clarity and ancestry — both useful for his current needs.

Even as Sandra handed over the charm, Max had to smirk. "Isn't it weird that we both know magic exists, we both use it, yet the idea of crystal and crystal therapy and all of that seems like New Age mumbo-jumbo?"

"It's a weird world, hon." She gave his chest a pat. "Now, go talk to the senile woman in the witch hospice."

Dropping his head back against the seat of his car, he let his eyes close. In the last few days, he had barely slept enough to add up to one good night. Though loath to admit it, his body did not seem to bounce back like it once had from pulling all-nighters. Not that he would let his mother know, but he made a mental note to start paying closer attention to his research habits — to not be afraid to call it a night. The work would still be there in the morning.

With a shake of his head, he opened his eyes and went up to the front door. Lee answered on the first ring. As she beamed a joyful greeting, he wondered if she had been watching him sit in the car, waiting for him to come up and ring the bell.

"Edith is going to be delighted to see you again." Lee said, heading toward the stairs. "And so soon after your last visit. I'll be honest with you — I didn't think you'd be back for several months at the earliest."

"I didn't get very far last time. I'm hoping that seeing me again might help jog her memory, get her more aware."

"That's a good thought. I hope luck is with you."

At the top of the stairs, Max noticed a second living room off to the side with a television blaring a daytime talk show. Last time, that door had been closed. In fact, several more doors along the hallway stood ajar. As they walked down, Max noted the doors were for occupied rooms and one for a bathroom.

When he reached Edith's room, he saw that she sat in her wheelchair staring out the half-window as if no time had passed from his previous visit. He stepped forward. A sharp shock hit his side and he jumped back.

"Everything okay?" Lee asked.

Max's side throbbed from the jolt as if he had bumped an electric fence. He started to inspect the doorway when he recalled the symbols drawn on the jamb — a ward of some kind. Rubbing his side, his hand brushed the charm in his pocket. *Of course.* If the ward had been designed to repel magic, it would react with a charm every bit as easily as a nefarious form of magic.

Hoping that the shock did not ruin Sandra's work, Max turned to Lee. "I'm fine. I had a thought, though. Would it be okay if you brought Edith into that television room we passed? Perhaps a change of scenery would help matters."

"That's a wonderful idea. Feel free to move her. Do you mind? I have other patients to attend to."

"Certainly," Max said.

After Lee entered another room, Max took off his coat and set it on the hallway floor. He entered Edith's room, unlocked her wheelchair, and brought her out. Grabbing his coat, he wheeled her down to the television room. He repeatedly watched around, expecting Lee or some other employee to jump out and accuse him of tampering with a patient or some other crime against the elderly.

When he had her settled, he shut off the television and closed the door. He brought out the charm and placed it in Edith's shaking hand. With one final check at the door, he closed her hand over the charm and pulled out a piece of paper Sandra had prepared. On it, she had written the phonetics for three words from a dead language he had never heard of.

Like an ancient monk, he lowered his head and whispered the words. He heard a soft crack like a dropped wine glass. Sandra said the charm might break once used but not to worry. Except if the charm cracked, then its effects would last a shorter time.

Peeking upward when he finished, he saw a coherent Edith Walker staring back. She wasn't smiling.

"Where am I?" She demanded more than asked. "Why aren't I in my room?"

"I'm Max Porter. I couldn't use a charm in your room, so I brought you here. I need information about back when you worked next to the funeral home. Back when you may have had something to do with Spaghetti Man."

Her eyes widened like a fawn caught before an oncoming car. "I must get back to my room. I'm not safe out here."

"I only need a name, and I can take you back."

She opened her mouth to call for help but snapped it shut just as fast. "Do they know I'm out?"

"Who?"

"Anybody who works here." She twisted her body in order to look behind her.

"Ms. Lee said I could take you to this room."

"Get me back to my room. You must. Please. It's the

only place I'm safe. The witches — they'll crack into my thoughts soon enough. You can't trust them."

Max took control of the wheelchair and turned Edith toward the door. But he stopped. "I'm sorry," he said. "I'll take you back, I will, but I need that name. I'm trying to help others and you're my only way forward. There's a petrified hand with a ring on it that —"

"You found the witch's hand?" Tossing her head from side to side, tears flowed down her cheeks. "You stupid boy. Leave that hand alone. Don't get involved any more than you are. You want nothing to do with this."

"What's so special about the hand?"

"No, no, no. There's no time. I must get back to my room. There are no wards out here."

"A name. That's all I need. The name of the witch whose hand you petrified."

Edith's constant motion turned into an exaggerated nod. "Kalinski. The witch's name was Danica Kalinski. Now, get me back to my room."

Max threw open the door and pushed Edith into the hallway. Lee stood in front of the door to Edith's room. She flashed her warm smile.

"There's no need for her to go back." Lee took a few steps closer. "She's welcome to spend the day out here with the rest of our patients."

"She's tired," Max said. "She'd like to rest." He heard chanting coming from the room that shared a wall with Edith's room.

"Don't be foolish. You got the information you wanted. She means nothing to you now. Leave her there in the hall. Go home. You won't be bothered."

Shaking his head while plastering a ridiculous smile on his face, Max said, "No, I'm afraid that's not going to happen."

Lee pressed her hands against her hips. "Oh? You think you can get by me?"

He had been wondering the same thing. But he did have an idea. He leaned over Edith and whispered, "Hold on tight. I'm going to get you to safety."

Edith gripped the arms of her chair. Max lowered his body and shoved off. Pumping his legs, he raced down the hall. Edith screamed. Max looked up in time to see Lee's face shift from defiance to shock to the realization that she had waited too long to move.

The wheelchair footrests stuck out front which meant that they hit first. Smacking right into Lee's shins, the sudden clash knocked Max forward. His arm reached out and barred Edith from popping out of the chair.

Lee cried out and tumbled backward. Blood oozed out of two large gashes in her shins. The door next to Edith's room swung open, and Max saw a circle of four elderly women chanting while holding red candles. A wrinkled and bent man held the door, his eyes taking in the scene.

Max pointed right at his face. "You take one step out here and I'll knock you on your ass."

The old man made a sour face and closed the door. Max pushed Edith into her room and fell onto her bed. After he caught his breath, he lifted his head. Edith gazed out the half-window.

"Edith? Can you hear me?"

No response, her mind lost once more.

He stood and stepped toward the hall but stopped. Would she be safe here? She had to be — she'd been living here for years. Whatever wards she had on this room — and Max thought there had to be more besides that one etched on the doorway — they were strong enough to keep her safe up to now.

When Max entered the hall, the old man had helped Lee

back to her feet. Her bright smile had vanished into an ruthless scowl. Her hands balled into tight fists. "What did she tell you?"

"Nothing," Max said, walking to the stairs. "She's out of her mind."

Lee followed, limping and thudding her way down the hall. "She told you something."

"She told me you witches want to hack into her mind. But I guess that's off the table since she's protected again." He stopped at the bottom of the stairs. Lee's bleeding shins meant she would have a hard time getting down with any speed, and he had no fear of the residents jumping him. He could outrun a gaggle of people using canes, walkers, and wheelchairs.

"We'll win this standoff — either by getting her now or waiting until she dies. All it takes is a fool like you wheeling her out for us."

Thinking back to his first visit, Max wagged his finger. "Her ward — it shocks you or something?"

"Or something."

"You've probably tried hiring somebody non-witchy to wheel her out."

Lee's jaw jutted to the side. "She nearly burned the place to the ground."

"I'm beginning to like Edith a lot more."

"Then help her out. Tell us what she told you. Did she name a witch? Anything she gave you would be helpful. Once we have what we want, there's no need for us to come after her anymore. We can let her live out the rest of her life in peace."

Max kicked the bottom stair. "I have a strong feeling that if I helped you, the rest of her life would be very short."

He walked to the front door. From the stairs, Lee

shouted, "You are making an enemy of powerful witches."

Over his shoulder, he shouted back, "Wouldn't be the first time."

Chapter 13

WITH THE DAY WANING, Max drove across town and parked near the office. He had a name — Danica Kalinski. It looked like a unique name, too. He crossed his fingers that researching Ms. Kalinski wouldn't be too difficult. How many Danica Kalinskis could there be in North Carolina? Or even the entire Unites States?

But as Max entered his office and shuffled off his coat, Drummond came sweeping through the walls. "Where's everyone been?" he said.

"Working." Max dumped the old coffee in the bathroom sink and went about preparing a fresh batch. "Where have you been?"

"The Other — like you asked."

"And?"

"And nothing. I told you it didn't look good. Aunt Holly isn't there."

Measuring out scoops of ground beans, Max said, "That took you all day? Usually, you're faster than that."

"I had things to do."

"It's a shame. You missed out on a lot of fun. That hospice turned out to be a home for old witches."

"Really?" Drummond moved in close. "Tell me about it."

"Later. Right now, I've got a name to follow up on — Danica Kalinski."

"Never heard of her. You want some help doing the research?"

Max paused to look straight at Drummond. "Okay, out

with it. What's the matter?"

"Nothing."

"If something is wrong, something bothering you, you can tell me. I'm your partner, after all."

Drummond drifted away from Max's view. "I'm fine. Can't I simply be offering to help on the research?"

Max whirled around. "No. You never want to hit the books with me."

"I still don't, but it's got to get done."

"You're being stubborn. It's obvious something has you upset."

"Are you so much of an idiot you can't tell that I got dumped?"

"Dumped?"

"Miss 1800s ran off with a dead singer from some 1960s one-hit wonder. Now you know. Satisfied?"

Setting up at his desk, Max wanted to say that he knew a deflection when he heard one — Drummond had taught him well on that part. But he simply dropped it. Something else bothered his ghost partner, but until Drummond wanted to talk about it, nothing would pry the information loose.

"None of my business. Sorry. You want to help research, let's get started." Max pulled three large books from the shelf and let them thud on the desk.

Drummond flinched. "You're going to be reading all of those?"

"Searching on the internet, too. If that doesn't produce results, then it's off to the library."

Drummond looked ill like he had swallowed a lizard. "You know, that stuff ain't really my strong spot. Maybe I should go back to the Other."

"You said Aunt Holly wasn't there."

"What about this Ruskie you're researching?"

"Danica Kalinski? Sure. Go in the Other. I doubt she's there, but you can check." If she were in the Other, she would have been causing Edith Walker a lot more trouble, and Edith would have needed far stronger wards. But, at least, it meant getting Drummond out of the office so Max could work in peace.

"I got it," Drummond said, zipping into the bookshelf. "Danica Kalinski. If she's in the Other, I'll find her."

Alone again, Max exhaled long and slow. He pushed down his rising concern over Drummond. He cared about his friend, but whatever troubled the ghost did not seem to be sending him toward poltergeist territory. And at least having a ghost for a partner meant not having to fear Drummond might commit suicide over some hidden secret. So, for the moment, Max needed to focus on his work.

After a few basic searches that he expected to be fruitless — for instance, googling Danica Kalinski on the off-chance that the witch had developed a legend or folklore around her — he decided to attack the problem backwards. Rather than find references to the woman's life, Max tried finding references to her death. Obituaries.

While he could not assume that it was Edith Walker who cut off the witch's hand, he thought it a good bet that Walker was the one who actually embalmed the hand. Based on the timing of her life crossing paths with the McDougald Funeral Home and Spaghetti Man, Max placed the hand incident somewhere around World War II. Though there was no guarantee Kalinski died at that time — she could have lived long after losing her hand — Max gambled she had died around then. Mostly because of what he had not found — evidence of the witch's activity.

Had she lived, she would have fought to regain her hand. Max had seen such behavior for other body parts. Plus, witches were not a forgiving bunch. Kalinski would have done something dramatic, something Max would have come across either in his research on this case or from his previous cases — especially, all the work he had done for the Hull family. At the time of losing her hand, Kalinski's life would have been governed by the Hulls — they once controlled all the magic usage in the area. Until they met Max.

He smiled inwardly. Taking down that family had been a point of pride for him. If nothing else, he had accomplished that much.

Sifting through the obituaries of Winston-Salem, Greensboro, and the smaller towns between, took Max deep into the night. He finally stumbled upon an entry dated July 27, 1941 in the *Winston-Salem Journal*.

Danica Kalinski. Though young in age, Danica lived a life fuller than most. She traveled the world and enjoyed all it had to offer. Few knew her well, but those she did bring into her circle became close confidants. She never married and had no children, but those women who cared about her considered her like a daughter. She will be greatly missed.
—PR

The initials *PR* sent Max into another hefty research binge. Two words stood out — mention of a circle and referring to those who cared about her solely as *women*. Knowing Kalinski was a witch gave these hints added weight. Enough that Max suspected Kalinski and PR to both have belonged to a coven.

As he flipped through pages of books and compared to information online, Max tried to find mention of these women. His main problem — covens didn't advertise their existence. Except for the more modern ones, and those tended to be more of the nature-loving Wiccan types than the full-on spell-casting witch types. However, a few covens of the kind he sought did keep an active online presence, including an ancestry. He searched those thoroughly.

At one point, he heard the office door open. Sandra and his mother entered. He heard Sandra whisper, "See? He's fine. He gets myopic like this when he's researching. Nothing to worry about."

"Will he remember to eat?" his mother said.

"He'll be fine. Let's go before we interrupt his thoughts."

They left, and his lips curled upward. He would have to do something extra-special for Sandra. She took good care of him.

Several hours later, he stared at a name on his screen, a short bio that went with it, and a listing of the same name in some old Hull records he had from previous research. Polly Rising. A fortune teller who appeared to have crossed paths with Danica Kalinski right before the 1929 stock market crash. The two relied on each other through the Great Depression, sharing an apartment owned by the Hull family and rented to both names.

"Got you," Max said. Now, all he had to do was research Polly Rising and see what turned up. That proved infinitely easier. Within two online searches, he fell upon a story that connected the fortune teller with a bizarre tale of murder.

Chapter 14

MAX DANCED ON THE BALLS OF HIS FEET as he paced the office. Sandra, the Sandwich Boys, Mrs. Porter, and Drummond had all assembled that morning after his call. Mrs. Porter and PB had brought in breakfast (bagels, donuts, and some fruit) while Jammer J brewed coffee and set up a buffet line on a card table he swiped from somewhere — Max didn't want to know. As both boys continued to vie for Mrs. Porter's attention, Max considered the benefits of the situation. A clean office and having other people set up breakfast meant a lot.

Drummond hung near the corner of the ceiling. His grim countenance suggested that nothing had improved for him. Max wanted to ask, but there was a limit to how much "talking at nothing" he could do in front of his mother.

Sandra munched on a chocolate-glazed donut while sitting behind her desk. "We're all here. How much longer are you going to draw this out?" She winked at Max.

He stuck his tongue out at her. "I'm getting there. I wanted everybody to have a chance to fuel up." He sipped on a hot mug of coffee. "Including me."

"Well, I ain't got all day," Drummond said. "Miss 1800 dumped 1960s. I got a source that said she missed me after only a few hours and knew she had made a mistake. Now, I'm not the kind to fall for a woman as indecisive as that, but I'll say this. She's a good looking ghost and I wouldn't mind a few playful hours."

Sandra choked on her donut, coughing hard. When she regained control, she drank some coffee to wash down the last of the donut. "Please, hon, let's get this started before anybody else starts chatting away."

"I think you're right." Max continued pacing as he spoke. "This took place in Fayetteville. It's a few hours east of here. Fort Bragg borders the city now and, not surprisingly, Laurinburg — home of the famous Spaghetti Man — is one of the nearby towns.

"Back in the 1840s, there was a beautiful girl —"

"Oh, come on," Drummond said. "You're saying it's my girl?"

"— named Ann Carver."

"Oh. Not my girl then. Good. Dodged that bullet."

"Ann had little money, her mother was a widow and ran a boarding house, but she had her looks, and back then, that meant everything for some women. She had fallen in love with a man, but before anything could come of that, her mother married her off to Alexander Simpson. This was in 1846. She was sixteen. He was in his early thirties."

Max checked his notes. "They moved into a two-story house on Gillespie Street near the Market House. Alexander ran a carriage shop, he had employees, and was well-regarded in the community. Other than his marriage to a child-bride, which at the time was not considered so terrible, his only real fault was a serious case of hypochondria.

"Two of his employees, Sam Smith and A. H. Whitfield, boarded at the Simpson home. That's important for later.

"Now, every description of Ann is positive. She was attractive, attentive, and agreeable. People liked her. The only person who seemed turned off by her was another sixteen-year-old girl who lived across the street — Miss Rachel Arey. However, most people thought Rachel's problem with Ann had more to do with Mr. Whitfield living under the same roof. She had a thing for Whitfield and probably didn't like the possibility that he might be taken in by Ann's charm. As a result, the two girls had a spat and remained formal around each other when forced to be in the same space.

"Those are all the people involved in this with the exception of Polly Rising, and I'll get to her in a minute."

PB and J sat on the floor, their faces covered in powdered sugar, and listened intently. Too often, Max forgot that these boys were actually still boys. Though he had no idea of their exact age, PB couldn't have been more than fifteen and J was a year or two younger. Despite their adult ways in many circumstances, moments like this reminded Max of how young they were in truth.

"Life started out okay for Ann and Alexander. Court records said little regarding how Ann felt about being married off, though later she did say that she only agreed to marry Alexander so she could have her own house. In the first two years together, Ann got pregnant twice. Both times, the infants died. She did not appear too shaken by this experience; however, with no money problems and three slaves in the house to take care of all the cooking, cleaning, and other chores, Ann had little to do each day. She took to daily walks.

"This went on for a while. Somewhere around 1849, she started to frequent Benbow's Factory Row — a less savory part of town. It's here that she became a loyal customer of the fortune teller, Polly Rising. Ann was known to get her fortune told several times a week. And, according to court testimony, Rising told Ann that she and Mr. Simpson would live together only five years." Tapping his notebook, Max added, "I forgot one person, Nancy Register. She was a seamstress who came to Ann's house every day to make clothes for Ann. The two became good friends, and often chatted away the hours together."

Mrs. Porter sniffled. "I don't really care for the way you characterize these women. I know I've taught you better than that."

"These are not my characterizations. Most of what I'm telling you comes from the court records. But it's important because it helps you understand the way people thought back then."

PB grabbed another donut. "People really married like that?"

"Yeah, they did. But that doesn't mean everybody was happy about it. Or that they stayed truthful. See, one day Ann came home to find a letter on the table. After reading it, she hurried to the sewing room where Nancy Register was working. And then she read it to Nancy. This is what it said:

Ann, I once thought you loved me, but now I have reason to suspect, that you love another better than me. For the sake of your friends, you may stay in my house, but you must find your own clothes as well as you can. Prepare a bed for me upstairs tomorrow. You can no longer be my wife.

Now, we have to take Nancy's word for it, but that was the note according to her. The original note had been tossed in the fireplace. According to Nancy, Ann decided to ignore the letter and treat her husband with extra affection. She confessed that her fortune teller had promised the marriage would end after five years and three were already used up. Ann figured she could last the rest."

Sandra raised her hand to get Max's attention. "Was she actually cheating or was Alexander paranoid?"

"We really only have Nancy's testimony to help us there, and it's not clear. There are references to a man named James who Ann said had the sweetest kisses of any man in the world."

J said, "Doesn't that say it all right there?"

"James could be the name of the man she had fallen for before being married off. When she talked of his kisses, it could be a reference to her memory of them, not to a recent event. It doesn't matter, though, because Alexander certainly believed she was cheating. After a mild reconciliation, he lost his temper and threw her out of the house. Shortly after that she came back. And then there was a quarrel that ended badly — at least, according to her.

"On October 25, 1849, she visited Polly Rising and told the fortune teller that her husband had beat her with his fist. Ms. Rising knew a lot more about the supernatural than simple fortune telling. She also did not like her clients being abused. But rather than give Ann the knowledge of witchcraft that Ms. Rising had been acquainted with, she told Ann about the marvelous properties of arsenic.

"Here the story gets both sensational and ridiculous. I can't figure out whether Ann's behavior was stupid and blatant to all around her or, because there were fewer examples to go by — no television crime shows, far fewer mystery novels — her behavior showed somebody who thought her plan would actually work. Either way, on November 3, Ann joyfully entered Samuel Hinsdale's drug store and asked for an ounce of arsenic. She claimed to have a rodent problem."

Mrs. Porter huffed. "I suppose nobody questioned her at all."

"Arsenic wasn't an uncommon request for dealing with rats."

"It couldn't have been that common either," she said. "But you can bet any amount of money that the person giving her the arsenic was a man. You said that she was a real beauty. By this point, she's maybe nineteen. I'm sure the deadest of souls would still be blinded by a seductive smile of a nineteen-year-old girl."

Max gave his mother a quick nod which she returned as if to say her comments settled the matter. He paused to make sure he still had the group's attention — including a glance upward at Drummond. "Four days go by before she arranges a noon meal for the house. Since her husband was there and apparently in good spirits, it's safe to assume that she spent some of those four days smoothing things over. The two boarders — Samuel Smith and A. H. Whitfield — also were there. Dessert was syllabub."

"What's that?" PB asked.

"I had to look it up. It's a strange concoction — usually milk or cream curdled with wine, cider or something like that. A little sugar or whipped cream and it's served as a drink or thickened and given like a custard. Of course, in the case of this particular meal, it is a good guess that there may have been some arsenic in one of the glasses.

"That night, the same group of people got together for some evening coffee. As Ann brought out the coffee, Mr. Smith took one of the cups. Ann commented but was not heard. She then reportedly said in a sharp voice that caused Mr. Smith to jump, 'I said that was Mr. Simpson's coffee.' Smith gave the coffee over and they all drank."

Sandra said, "Not very subtle."

"It gets worse. After drinking, Ann takes her husband's cup and plays the Polly Rising game by reading his fortune in the coffee grounds. She says, 'I see a sick bed, a coffin, and a dark and muddy road with clouds around.' She went on with references to the fortune she had been given numerous times that predicted Alexander's death.

"This talk soured the evening for Alexander, and he claimed to be feeling ill. Now remember, he was a known hypochondriac, so nobody gave him a second thought. The next morning, however, Alexander was suffering in bed. Ann sent for Dr. William Mallett. Though the doctor attempted to administer comfort — eventually using morphine — the pain grew worse. Ann tried to be at his side, but Alexander verbally lashed out at her.

"Ann opted to take care of her boarders. She prepared a noonday meal, and acted the proper host to Smith and Whitfield. But then, in the middle of their conversation, she asked Smith about the effect of arsenic on rats."

Mrs. Porter clicked her tongue. "This girl is an idiot. I mean you can only rely on your looks to get you so far."

"She certainly wasn't as clever as she thought. As the slow death continued, her behavior never became that of a concerned wife. Around nine o'clock that night, Alexander fell into a coma and died. Rather than falling into tears, Ann found herself chatting with the neighbor Miss Rachel Arey."

J said, "Isn't she the one Ann hated?"

"That's right. Yet Ann couldn't stop her mouth. She confided in Rachel that she had been seeing Polly Rising and told of the fortune teller's prediction. I suppose Ann thought this would bolster her case, but of course, the only reason we know these conversations happened is because it all ended up in court testimony. So, Ann flubbed that whole thing.

"Dr. Mallett asked Ann for permission to conduct an autopsy. She had the sense to agree — what else could she do? — and it was all downhill from there. One look at Alexander's stomach and Dr. Mallett knew. The justice system went into action, and soon Judge John Dick issued a bench warrant for Ann Simpson. But they couldn't find her. She had fled.

"She was gone for a year. And then shows up, ready to turn herself in provided that she received an immediate trial. She claimed that she ran only out of fear of being stuck in prison for months while they got the court case together." Max had detailed notes of the trial, it was a bombastic experience, but he could tell the boys were getting antsy. "In the end, the jury — all men who could not believe such a sweet, innocent looking gal could do such a horrid deed — they found her not guilty."

"She got away with it?" Sandra said.

Mrs. Porter said, "Of course, she did. I could have told you that before Max had gotten a minute into this."

Max closed his notebook. "Once free, she left Fayetteville. I guess she decided she knew how to get away with killing a husband because she turns up in the news some years later. This time in *The Milwaukee Sentinel*. Unfortunately for her, that trial did not go as smoothly. She was executed in St. Paul for killing her then husband, Mr. Bilansky."

"This is all fascinating," Drummond said with more growl in his voice than Max wanted to hear, "but what's this got to do with Kalinski's hand and the Dardens?"

Trying not to talk to the ceiling, Max said, "The last bit of interest here is that Polly Rising disappeared right after Alexander Simpson died. I guess she had a premonition that things were going to go badly for her if she stuck around."

Stretching her arms, Sandra said, "Good work, hon."

"Not really," he said. He sat at his desk, glowered at his notebook, and tapped his chin. "The hand is only loosely connected to this story through Polly Rising because much, much later — during The Great Depression, she's in her nineties and ends up living with Kalinski. And nothing notable turns up for any of the names involved before Ann's marriage. I hate to say it, but after all that work, this might be nothing more than an interesting story. I think we've hit another dead end."

While Mrs. Porter and the Sandwich Boys cleaned up breakfast, Drummond dropped into the center of the room. "Well, that's dandy, isn't it? You spent all this time with your head in books and yet you got nothing to show for it."

Max clamped his mouth shut. Drummond knew it would be difficult for anybody to talk back to him, and he took full advantage of that fact.

"This case has been nothing but one red herring after another. How the hell are we to stop evil things from happening when the deck is stacked? Huh? I've devoted my life to this crap and all that ever happens is you get dumped on more."

"You're the one who convinced me to take this case," Max said. His mother's head perked up. She must have thought he berated Sandra, and perhaps she hoped to witness a fight.

Sandra stood, planted her hands on her desk, and said in slow, hard tone, "Let's calm down. All of us."

"Doll," Drummond said, his voice lacking his usual charm, "I ain't got time for calm. This case has been going down the drain from the start. So both of you need to figure something out."

"What about you?" Max said.

"I'm going to do some real detective work."

Drummond soared out through the window. Sandra walked across the office until she stood beside Max. She lowered her head and whispered, "We can't let him go off like that."

"We can't really stop him," Max whispered back.

"No, but I might be able to track him. There's a basic spell used to locate people or items. I imagine there must also be a spell for locating ghosts. At least, we'll be able to find out where he's gone."

He never liked asking Sandra to cast spells, but he saw no other choice. They needed to help Drummond — not only because he was a tremendous asset to the team but because he was their friend. He nodded. "What do you need?"

She cocked her head in the direction of Mrs. Porter. "I need time alone."

He thought for a moment when he noticed the silence in the office. His mother and the boys had stopped cleaning up. They watched him as a pack might watch the alpha, waiting for a sign of what was to happen next.

Max stood. To his wife, he asked, "You said you can locate items, right?"

"That's what it's supposed to do. I've never tried it."

"Good enough." To the others, he said, "So, I didn't get to finish."

"There's more story?" PB asked as he tied up a half-full garbage bag.

"No. But while I said that the lead seemed to go nowhere, I have an idea of something we can try. I'll need some help."

Both PB and J straightened up. "We're ready," J said.

"What are we doing?" Mrs. Porter asked. "You're not getting these boys into trouble, are you?"

"Trouble? Not at all." Max walked over to the group. "We're going back to the Darden house. I'm going to give them a report on my findings."

"And?"

He grinned. "And we're going to steal Aunt Holly's journal."

Chapter 15

As Mrs. Porter drove up toward the Darden mansion, Max's fingers tapped rapidly on his knee. The day had gone quickly, and as evening approached, he questioned the entire plan. Feeling nervous was nothing new, but having so much to be nervous about — that turned his stomach.

He felt nervous for Sandra as she mined her sources to learn a spell for locating ghosts. Magic could be temperamental, and for a novice, it could be dangerous. Worst of all for Max, he couldn't do anything to help other than get out of the way.

He felt nervous about Drummond. That ghost had more secrets than most of their clients. Every time Max thought he knew Drummond well, another secret unearthed. It wouldn't be so bad if he didn't have to constantly count on Drummond.

But mostly, Max felt nervous because he never had been put in this situation before — having to fully rely on his mother and the Sandwich Boys. In the past, they had been part of a larger plan, but always Sandra and Drummond were involved, too. This time, it was just them.

Trying to follow one of the many lessons Drummond had given, Max did his best to keep the plan simple. The simpler the plan, the easier to improvise when things went wrong. Also if possible, make sure that each person had a single task to focus on.

He assigned his mother to be the driver. He didn't see any reason they would have to speed away, but it was a task both singular and simple. Plus, it kept his mother from getting too involved — she had made it clear that she liked to be part of a case but not too much.

The Sandwich Boys had riskier jobs, starting with PB who exited the car with Max. They approached the front door, walking by the massive pillars. Placing a hand on his shoulder, Max said, "Try not to walk around with your mouth gaping open."

PB snapped his mouth shut, but his eyes remained wide open, roving around the daunting mansion.

Max rang the bell and they waited. Mrs. Porter turned the car around in the open courtyard. She kept her eyes focused ahead as if ready to bolt the second she heard burglar alarms. Max chuckled.

The front door opened and Chelsea Darden appeared. "Why, hello there. What an unexpected surprise." She bent closer to PB. "Who is this fine looking gentleman?"

Max said, "This is PB. He's sort of an intern, sort of a protégé."

"Impressive for such a young man. I gather you're here with news, so come on in. We were just sitting down to supper."

As they followed Chelsea through the maze of halls to the dining room, Max's mouth watered at the tasty aroma floating through the air. They entered a cavernous hall with marble floors that echoed the click of Chelsea's heels. Instead of a long table capable of seating twenty guests, the Dardens opted for a normal, dark wood dining table — rectangular and designed for six. It took center stage but looked tiny on the mostly empty floor.

Grandma Darden's wheelchair had been positioned at the head while the siblings each had a place on the sides. Golden-brown duck and bright vegetables had been served on beautiful, china plates while wine filled delicate, crystal glasses.

"Would you care to join us?" Chelsea said.

PB stepped toward the table, but Max snagged his shirt to stop him. "No, thank you. We won't be long. I simply wanted to report in with an update."

Lane perked up. "Does that mean you can break this spell? I'm getting bored stuck here all day."

Snickering, PB said, "Spell?"

Max bumped his shoulder against PB. Someday soon, he would have to teach the boy about the real world — the supernatural world. "Not yet, but we're getting closer to the truth. Once we know who did this to you and why, we'll have little trouble setting you free. It's all in the details. In fact, as we speak, my associates are researching possible spells and those with the ability to cast such things."

After a pause, Alan set his fork onto his plate. He wore a dress shirt and a sports coat making him look more like a banker than the guy with an early mid-life crisis Max had seen before. Alan said, "Is that it? You came all the way out here to tell us that you haven't found anything yet?"

"No, of course not. I was hoping to speak with Ms. Chelsea privately for a moment."

Lane and Alan both turned toward Chelsea. Her face reddened. She forced a smile. "I'm sure whatever you want to ask me can be said in front of everybody. We have nothing to hide."

"Lady," PB said, "everybody's always got something to hide."

Max swallowed down the urge to reprimand PB into silence. Instead, he rested his hand on PB's shoulder and tightened his grip until the boy inched back. "Ms. Chelsea, I appreciate the openness you have with your family. It's admirable. However, in my line of work discretion is often an important aspect to solving a case. If you'll allow me this indulgence, I'd like to speak with you in private — perhaps we can go to the library — and if afterwards, you feel that I'm being overly cautious, then go right ahead and tell the family as much as you want."

Lane and Alan continued to stare at Chelsea. Alan raised his eyebrows to underscore whatever unspoken conversation appeared to be going on.

"Oh, very well," Chelsea said, snapping her napkin to the side before folding it and placing it next to her plate. As she stood, her chair scraped against the floor and the sound bounced around the walls like a moaning ghost.

"Thank you," Max said and walked off toward the library. He made sure to be in the lead so that Chelsea could not alter their course to some other room. Once inside, he said, "I apologize if I embarrassed you, but I wasn't sure how much the others knew."

"About what?"

"The petrified hand you showed me. Would you please bring it in here? I'd like to take a few pictures, so I can refer to it back at the office. I believe that hand is going to be crucial to this case."

Her brow loosened, and her forced grin no longer looked forced. "That old thing? Why didn't you say so? I told you. We don't have secrets. Lane and Alan know about the hand. It's not a big deal."

"Then I can take some pictures?"

With a relieved giggle, she said, "Certainly. I'll go get it."

After she left, Max counted to three. Then he turned to the nearest stack and raced through the titles. PB hurried to the door, closed it most of the way, and pressed his face close to the crack.

It had taken Sandra several hours to pull off the spell that located Aunt Holly's journal, but it had worked. She found the journal in the Darden library. Unfortunately, Sandra's skill did not reach the level of pinpointing exactly where in the library. But Max had seen the journal before. He knew what it looked like. He could find it.

He hoped.

"Hey, Ghostman," PB said in a loud whisper. Ever since he first found out that Max thought he talked to a ghost, PB called him Ghostman. "I'm not complaining here, but I'm curious. Why are you ripping off these folks?"

Max had no time to stop, but he knew PB well enough. When the boy latched onto something, he rivaled an angry dog in letting go. So, while Max combed through the stacks, he tried to give PB some part of his brain. "I'm not ripping them off."

"Come on, man. I don't care what scam you're running here. I'm not judging. I just don't get it. You never did this kind of thing before. I mean, these folks are nuts. If they weren't rich, they'd have been locked up long ago. Talking spells and curses. And you're here telling them that you can save them from it all."

Max shifted to the next aisle of books. "I would've thought you'd have a more open mind by now. You've been with us for a handful of cases. Are you telling me this is the first weird thing you've heard us talking about?"

"No, but before you were dealing with a cult. Cults believe all kinds of wacko crap. And the other cases were rather bland. I mean, I'm sure almost dying in a house fire wasn't bland to you, but you've done a clear job of keeping me and J away from the main action. You telling me all those cases dealt with crazy people like this?"

Max climbed the rolling ladder to look over the second floor books. Most of those shelves had a thin layer of dust. He dismissed them and focused on those that looked recently disturbed.

"This world is a big place," Max said.

"I seen a lot of the world. Believe me."

"You've seen a lot of the streets of Winston-Salem. You know parts of the world that most people never have to deal with. In fact, if you were to go back into that dining room and tell those folks eating duck about the things you've witnessed since you were little — eight, right? — they'd think you were lying. No way could an eight-year-old endure the life you've led. But that's because the world they know and the world you know are two different places."

As he continued his search, he heard a thoughtful silence from below. At length, PB said, "You trying to say that all this spell talk is real? I don't mean really real, I mean it's real to them. Right? The rich people's world is different than mine, so what they see as magic is simply something I haven't bumped into yet. Is that it?"

"Something like that." Max scurried down the ladder. "Still clear?"

"Yup, but I wouldn't think you got much more time. It can't take that long for this lady to get a box from a room."

"It's a big house, but I think you're right."

Max moved toward the stacks near the far wall but stopped. He had been an idiot. When Lane snatched the journal from him, she didn't replace it neatly in the spot it came from. She didn't want him looking at it. She brought it to the library. But hiding it amongst books here would have been obvious when she knew he would be coming back to the house until the case had ended. If she really didn't want him to see the journal, she would make sure he could never stumble upon it again.

Perhaps there was a secret floorboard or a wall panel, but he didn't have time to search for that. Leaning back he tried to think of where he might hide a special book. He crossed his arms and lowered his head. That's when he saw that he had been resting on the edge of the oversized desk.

"Seriously?" he said.

Max rushed around to the opposite side and tried the drawers. Two on the right side opened with ease. One contained files and the other had pens, envelopes, staples, and other supplies. On the left side, Max found a top drawer filled with an appointment book and more clerical materials. Beneath the drawer, he saw a cabinet door — locked.

"Hurry up," PB said. "I hear voices."

Max opened the drawer on the right and shuffled things around until he saw a letter opener. Desk locks were rarely of a serious nature. He had seen this kind of thing jimmied open in the movies, and while he knew better than to judge anything based on a movie, he could think of no other option at the moment.

Licking his drying lips, Max stuck the letter opener in the gap between door and desk. He slid the blade downward until he felt it hit the lock. He pushed but the metal wouldn't give. Repositioning his body parallel with the desk, he put his weight into his efforts. Still nothing.

From the corner of his eye, he saw PB making circular *Hurry!* motions. Max's pulse hammered. He ripped the letter opener out and started at the bottom. This time when he hit the lock, he yanked upward and felt the metal spring out of place. The small door cracked open.

First thing he saw — a safe with a digital key code lock. His heart sank. But as he shifted his feet, the light hit so that he caught a glimpse of the journal — carefully pushed between the side of the safe and the wood of the desk. Using the letter opener, he snagged the top of the journal's binding and fished it out.

"Got it," he said.

PB made a cutting motion as he fast-walked toward Max. *Crap.* Chelsea entered the library carrying the cardboard box from the bedroom.

The original plan was for Jammer J to wait outside, below the library window, and Max would toss him the journal. J would then hurry to the car and wait for PB and Max. Should anything go wrong, J and Mrs. Porter could leave with the journal.

But Max had to stuff the journal in his coat pocket. He had no way to get to the window, no way to signal Jammer J that things had gone wrong, and no way to get out of the house with ease. It was possible that he might simply leave and nobody would be the wiser. However, his coat pockets were small, and the journal clearly poked out. At the moment, Chelsea's attention focused on the petrified hand, but when they left, anybody that offered a handshake or simply looked casually at Max would see the journal.

"Won't they know you took it when they find it gone later?" Jammer J had asked when Max explained the plan.

"Yes, they will. But they won't be able to directly say anything without admitting to its importance. That's a can of worms they don't want to open. If they did, they wouldn't be hiding the journal. But if they catch me stealing it, then they never have to explain anything. The spotlight will shift to accusations against me."

Max looked to PB who had moved out of Chelsea's way. She set the box on the desk. "Oof. You wouldn't think that'd be so heavy. But it takes its toll when you have to walk across the entire house."

"I suppose you should have a mini-golf cart to drive from one end to the other." Max's faux-jovial tone was matched by Chelsea's overenthusiastic laughter.

"Mr. Porter, you tease me. Anyway, here's the hand."

She brought out the glass cube and rested it on the desk.

PB brought the back of his hand to his forehead. "Oh. That's disgusting."

"Are you okay?" Chelsea asked, turning toward the boy.

"I'm sorry, Boss. I didn't think that hand would bother me." He walked over to Max and tripped at the last moment. Falling into Max's arms, he snatched the journal.

Great move, kid! Max rubbed PB's back, using his body to block Chelsea's view. "There, there. Why don't you go over to the window and get some air? I'll take the photos and put the hand away."

Chelsea picked up a wastepaper basket. "Are you going to throw up?"

Max intervened. "He'll be fine. Don't worry. I've seen this before. He just needs some air."

Stumbling across the library while keeping the journal clutched to his stomach, PB navigated his way to the window. He opened one of the low panels and leaned out.

"Please, Ms. Chelsea," Max said, pulling her attention away from PB. "If you'll hold the cube at an angle so I don't get any glare from the lights."

"Of course," she said.

Max brought his camera app up on his phone and purposely positioned across the table. In order to help him, Chelsea had to put her back to PB. As Max took his pictures, he saw PB close the window and give a thumbs up. Three more pictures — ones he actually needed — and they were done.

"Sorry about that," PB said, returning to the desk.

Chelsea pointed at him. "Stop right there."

Max and PB froze.

"The hand is still out," she said. "I don't want you getting sick again."

"All done," Max said, pocketing the phone. "This will be a tremendous help."

Chelsea packed away the hand. "Anything you need. I really want to be finished with all of this magic nonsense. Okay, young man. All clear here."

As they walked back to the foyer with its stained-glass dome and giant carpet underneath, Max felt his heartbeat slowing to a normal rhythm. Sweat trickled down his side, but he didn't think he looked bad or nervous. If he did, nobody made any acknowledgment of the fact.

Alan pushed Grandma Darden across the foyer, heading for the living room. "Next time you come here," he said, "please do the polite thing and call first. We missed our sister for the entire meal, and since you obviously did not solve our problem, that was an unnecessary intrusion."

"My apologies," Max said.

Watching Grandma Darden's blank eyes as she rolled by, Max thought of Edith Walker. He wondered which would be worse — being stuck in a wheelchair surrounded by only a few family members in a large empty house or being stuck in a wheelchair surrounded by numerous old strangers in an overcrowded facility. Neither sounded pleasant.

Lane gamboled by, making a straight dive for her tablet and the couch while Chelsea opened the front door. "Goodnight, Mr. Porter. Please let us know if there's anything else we can do to help."

"Of course. Goodnight."

Max forced himself to walk at a normal, casual pace, and PB followed suit. When they reached the car, they settled in. Mrs. Porter gently pressed the gas, and though every fiber of Max wanted to scream, he merely rested his head against the passenger side glass and waited.

He did not move again until they left the Darden property. At that point, he spun around in the seat and put his hand out. "J, give me the journal."

Like a drug addict, he snatched the journal and started looking at it. But then he paused. He inhaled, held it, and exhaled. "Mom, boys — thank you. You all did a fantastic job."

"No problem," PB said. "I hope you get something good out of it."

Max let his hand brush over the cover of the journal. "Me, too."

Chapter 16

MAX THOUGHT ABOUT GOING BACK to the office, but his body rejected the mere hint of pulling another all-nighter. Pointing out the heavy bags under his eyes, Max's mother dropped him off at the house and said she would see the boys safely to their apartment. Based on the devilish grins covering PB and J's faces, Max had a feeling they might stop to get some ice cream along the way. At the rate his mother plowed ice cream down their throats, he would have to look into a good dental plan for them.

Sandra sat on the living room floor with two books on witchcraft open before her. She wrote in a notebook balanced on her legs. Situated on their ottoman, she had her laptop with a website featuring a cartoon witch in the header displayed. As he closed the front door, she paused her studies.

"How'd it go?"

He patted the journal. "How about you?"

Dropping her pen onto the notebook, she said, "Okay, I guess. I wish there were a clearer answer, but witches and ghosts don't often work together."

"Drummond did okay once."

"If by *okay* you mean that he fell in love with a witch who came back from the grave to nearly destroy us all."

"True. There's that."

"And he was alive when he and Patricia were in love. No ghosts were involved at the time."

"I get it. Ghosts and witches don't get along. I take it then that there aren't a lot of spells between the two — in a co-operative way."

"Not even a playful, gag-gift kind of spell. Though there are plenty of ways to curse and destroy ghosts."

Max made a show of weighing the options. "I think that might be a tad overboard for our needs. We only want to find him."

"I will. Don't worry."

"I'm not. I trust you'll figure it out."

After washing up and putting on pajama bottoms and a t-shirt, Max shimmied under the covers of his bed. He held the journal on his chest. Part of him wanted nothing more than to spend a few hours reading whatever Aunt Holly had to offer. Part of him wanted to close his eyes.

As he debated the best course of action, the bedroom door opened. Sandra entered, resting her arm up the length of the door. "So, your mom is taking care of the boys right now."

Max's heart picked up its pace. "Could be a little bit before she gets back."

"That's what I'm thinking. And while I don't mind her staying here —"

"Oh?"

Sauntering toward the bed, she said, "Maybe I mind a little, but I understand."

"You are a very understanding person." Max set the journal on his nightstand.

"So, while she's been staying here, I've noticed a significant drop off in our time together."

As she placed on knee on the corner of the bed, Max grinned. "I don't know what you mean. We're together at the office every day."

Leaning forward so that he could glimpse her breasts, she said, "There's other kinds of together time that we need to share."

While Max was happy to continue this teasing banter, Sandra's statement held more truth than he cared to admit. He had been suppressing the masculine, testosterone driven side of himself for too long. It felt like months since they had last enjoyed each other. Watching her crawl across the bed, seeing that happy twinkle and that hungry desire in her eyes drained the blood from his face as it all rushed further south.

When she pressed her lips against his, he closed his eyes and focused on the soft, wonderful sensation. Inhaling, he let her gentle scent fill his lungs. When he looked at her, when they smiled at each other, when he took her in his arms, he let out a low moan of relief.

"It's been too long," he said.

Before she could answer, they heard the front door open. Mrs. Porter had returned. Sandra arched her head back and let out a low moan of her own — disappointment.

"Damn," Max said, releasing his wife and sitting up in bed. "Of all the nights to skip on the ice cream."

He reached for the journal, but Sandra grabbed his hand. She pulled him back and rested his palm on her breast. With a raised eyebrow, he questioned her. She kissed him as she swung a leg over to straddle his body. When she pulled back, she raised one finger to her lips.

As excited as he had been when she first entered the bedroom, Max's heart tripled its beat seeing that she still wanted him — albeit as quietly as they could manage. She removed her blouse, leaned close, and all thoughts left his brain. Only Sandra remained.

* * * *

Around three-thirty in the morning, Max stared at the ceiling. He wished he could fall back asleep, but he knew better. Sex had relaxed him and exhaustion had claimed a few hours, but his mind could only rest for so long. Not wanting to bother Sandra — her soft snores brought a warm sensation over him — he picked up the journal and tiptoed his way down to his study.

Under the dim light of a single desk lamp, he opened the journal and read. The first thing to become clear was that this would be no ordinary journal. Aunt Holly had no interest in recording the daily activities of the Darden family nor did she want to ponder the mundane aspects of her life. If anything, the journal appeared to be a sounding board for her to weigh the value of each child under her care. She saw these kids like no other — not only because she was their guardian but because she had a keen eye for picking up subtle clues between them. All of her observations centered around which of these children would help return the craft of magic back under the Darden family name. And she wrote all of it down.

Her earliest entries focused on Chelsea. She wrote:

The girl is eager to please and easy to anger, though she hides it well. Often, I only notice a twitch of her eye or a tightness in her lips. Those are the singular marks to the anger boiling in her heart, often due to some minor slight from her siblings or a decision of mine she deems unfair.

Her confusion and distress pushes her to eat. The sweeter, the better. But I should not mistake this for weakness. It's easy to dismiss her. However, she is the first born Darden of her generation which brings with it a stronger blood tie to our hidden talents. Yet her hatred towards witchcraft may be bolder than the urges of her blood.

What a sad way to live, denying your true self out of fear or any reason.

She is a conflicted mess. Of course, some behavior problem is to be expected. She did lose both parents in a single, tragic night. But she's too old to fall for the car accident story. She knew where her mother's heart longed to be. No matter the fights, the denials, no matter how many times my sister claimed to be done with it all, she always returned. Chelsea's smart enough to understand that her parents did not perish under natural circumstances. And so, she's angry and bitter towards witchcraft. Whether I can change her opinion over time remains to be seen. At least now, I am the sole heir to the Darden fortune. The money will help build a strong foundation for the magic that we build.

"Holy crap," Max said to the book. He didn't know where to begin in his head — Aunt Holly admitting that the parents had been killed through magic or the twisted way Aunt Holly planned to profit from the deaths.

On the top of the next page, centered and capitalized, Aunt Holly had written ALAN. Underneath, she wrote:

Alan is a petulant boy. I suppose all boys are, but he is particularly talented at annoying me to no end. His emotions can shift drastically. Were it not for the death of his parents, I would have assumed he suffered from manic-depression or some similar mental ailment. But under the circumstances, I think he is merely trying to come to terms with his loss. Unfortunately, for me, on a good day, that often manifests in the form of pranks at my expense. On a bad day, it means tantrums, crying, hitting, screaming, anything to let out the rage.

It is a shame he's a boy. Were he a girl, I would see great potential and strength. I would choose him above all the siblings to teach him

*the ways of magic and our family obligation to the craft. But regardless
of the arguments, I am a firm believer that witchcraft was, is, and
shall always be a matriarchal magic by and for women. No doubt
discovered by a desperate wife under the oppressive thumb of an
abusive husband.*

Finally, on a new page under the heading LANE, Aunt
Holly wrote:

*An infant with no memory of her parents, Lane might be my best
chance at shaping a true soul to spark the revival of the Darden
family. But she might end up another disappointment. I'll have to wait
a few years until she's old enough to reveal her true self.*

In the pages that followed, Aunt Holly outlined and
detailed various moments and incidents as if she were a
lawyer presenting evidence to a court. But, as judge also,
she would eventually have to review her notes and make a
ruling. Max wondered how much of the distribution of
Aunt Holly's Will reflected that ruling.

Reading the journal further, it emerged that the children
were keenly aware of Aunt Holly's constant observation —
perhaps even aware of the trial going on in these pages.
Max swallowed a bitter taste.

Aunt Holly did little to referee the triangle of hate
created between the three children. In the journal, she
detailed how Lane and Chelsea would gang up on Alan one
day, and the next Alan and Chelsea would terrorize Lane.
Not to be outdone, Lane would employ Alan to have
revenge upon Chelsea. Back and forth, the three allied with
each other in a never-ending effort to control the odd one
out. For her part, Aunt Holly only intervened when their
actions disturbed the peace of the house.

One entry, however, stood out amongst them all.

Strange how the world never stops. People live and die. Empires are formed and crumble. A great President runs the country only to be replaced by an incompetent twit, and the incompetent President is replaced with a great one. Or, at least, a good one. Around and around. Atrocities are committed and wonderful sacrifices are made. Altruism comes in and out of fashion. All of it passes along, yet we always feel that our moment in time is crucial, special, different from all the other repetitions of these unending cycles. And so it is that a powerful weapon of magic that once was a prized possession of our family has returned to us.

If not for the internet, I might never have connected with the seller. Yet technology, a magic all its own, brought us together. The hand of Danica Kalinski.

I sit here writing this while I stare at the marvelous thing. I could see that Chelsea respected its power without even knowing what it represented or what is was for. Alan showed little interest, as usual. But Lane, there was an interesting reaction. Perhaps I've underestimated that child. I'd begun to think that she was like her sister, but I see now that she is ripe for molding in any direction I wish. It would certainly be easier than breaking through Chelsea's impenetrable walls. That child has simply decided to reject all I have to offer. I tire of fighting with her. But Lane. I'll have to think on that.

If she can be trained, then I'll have somebody in this family who can finally serve our greater purpose. I'll give her Kalinski's hand, and she will ...

Max looked at the next page — empty. He flipped through the rest of the journal. All of it — empty. He checked back on the final written page. Had he missed some scrawled sentence in the margins? No. But in the spine, he did see the jagged edges where two pages had been ripped out.

He stared at them for a full minute before snapping the journal shut. "Son of a bitch."

Chapter 17

SHORTLY AFTER THE SUN ROSE, Sandra shuffled into the kitchen, bleary-eyed and rumpled. From his office chair, Max watched her go through the motions of starting the morning coffee and pulling out a few eggs from the refrigerator. Each movement of her hands, the tilt of her head, and the way her nightshirt clung to her shape — it all brought back flashes of their youth.

She jumped and let out a short yip when she noticed him. "Don't do that," she said but laughed. "I almost dropped the eggs."

"You look so beautiful, I didn't want to stop you."

"You're not looking so hot. Didn't you sleep at all last night?"

"I had a good few hours." He grinned. "You had a lot to do with that."

Sandra pointed toward the ceiling. "Watch it. I think she's awake."

"I think I'm going up to bed." He pushed the journal across the desk. "We're screwed over yet again." He explained the overall purpose of the journal and how the final two pages — probably the most important pages — had been removed.

"Now I know you haven't had enough sleep. You're not thinking straight."

"What did I miss?"

Cracking the eggs into a bowl, she said, "How did you get that journal?"

"PB and I stole it."

"From?"

"The Darden house. Why are you asking things you know the answer to?"

"How did you know where the journal was?"

Max smacked his forehead. "Because you found it with a spell. You think you can find the missing pages, too?"

"Spells get easier once you've done them a few times. Let's have some breakfast and I'll get to it. Shouldn't take me nearly as long now that I know what I'm doing."

Max thought of his comfortable bed. "How long? Do I have time to get a little shuteye?"

"Definitely."

With a grateful kiss, Max skipped the eggs and went straight to his bed. Knowing Sandra had the next step in the case well under control, he found sleep easy to achieve. Unfortunately, the peace did not last long.

After what felt like minutes but had actually been two hours, Sandra shook him awake. He moved his groggy head to the side until his eyes focused on his wife. Then he bolted upright. "Where are the pages?" He saw the answer on her grim face. "You couldn't find them."

"I did and didn't find them. I mean, I didn't find them but not because I couldn't, not because the spell didn't work. I didn't find them because they don't exist anymore. Those pages have been destroyed."

Max pictured Chelsea tearing out the journal pages and tossing them in one of the numerous fireplaces of the mansion. He saw the orange light flickering on her face, the sadistic smile and trembling lips, the twitch that told Aunt Holly all she needed to know. Alan stood in the back with Lane, watching carefully as they destroyed the evidence Max needed.

But why would they hire him only to stymie every avenue that would help him break their curse?

"It doesn't matter," he muttered to himself. Louder, he said, "I think we've finally lost."

"Come on, hon. We've dealt with tougher cases than this."

"I can't think of one. Others were more dangerous, but at least I could research a name or a place and have it lead to more information. At least I could find a clue or two that would guide us to the answers. But this case." He shook his head. "That journal was going to be the answer. I can't think of another way to go forward. If Drummond were here, I'd tell him to quit. This is no good. And where is he, anyway? Usually we can't get rid of him, but this case, he's nowhere to help."

"Where's all this defeatist attitude coming from? I don't get it."

"How can you not feel this way? Name one thing that's gone right on this case. Heck, name one thing that's gone right since we moved to Winston-Salem."

Sandra smacked Max's arm. "Drummond, PB, J, this house, our financial security, our marriage is stronger, we have our independence — which we had to fight hard for — should I go on?"

Swinging his legs out of the bed, Max said, "Okay, okay. I'm not defeatist. I'm just frustrated. We've always done a good job at solving our problems by pushing through them. But this time, I can't see the way through. I keep thinking I've found it, but then ..."

"Missing pages in a journal."

"Exactly. What I really need right now is the expert opinion of a seasoned detective, but ours doesn't seem too co-operative lately."

"Then we need to help him deal with whatever his problem is, so he can help us with ours. And to do that, we need to find him. So, I'm going to cast my spell and figure out where he is."

Max rubbed his temples. "I thought you didn't know how to locate a ghost. Isn't that what all your research was about?"

"That's right. And after living with you all these years, I've picked up a few things in how to research. While I can't guarantee the outcome, I've cobbled together a spell that should show us Drummond's whereabouts. Or I'm wrong and the whole thing will fizzle and the house will smell like rotten eggs or sweaty feet for a few days."

"You better get it right, then. I don't want to deal with my mother's complaints about that kind of odor."

While Sandra went through the work of locating Drummond, Max forced himself to re-read the journal. Perhaps he had missed an entry or a significant comment. But nothing new jumped out at him as crucial.

His mind recounted all that he knew about the Dardens. They were stuck in their house, but it was worse than that. Even without the spell against them, they were stuck. Ghosts of their family's past haunted the grounds. Sandra had seen them. If Aunt Holly had ever succeeded in reintroducing serious magic to their family, they might see those dead slaves, too. Living on a plantation would fast lose its fairy tale rewrite of history.

"Probably a good thing," he said, his thumb playing with the corner of the journal.

But history was a double-edged sword. To ignore it meant to repeat the same mistakes. Yet to dwell within it meant to romanticize those same mistakes.

It seemed that Aunt Holly had walked the tightrope between these two ideas. She wanted to bring back magic, harken back to the days when she thought her family powerful and great. However, she ignored the tragic losses caused by the dangers of magic.

Grandma Darden should have been a daily reminder. After all, that woman had to be a witch. No way would Max believe anything else. Not after meeting Edith Walker.

Though he continued to think through the case, he knew his energy was wasted. He needed Drummond's input.

Hours later, Sandra finally called for Max. She sat on the living room floor. Sweat dappled her forehead and she had a faraway gaze in her eyes. Pointing to a maps program she had brought up on her computer, she said, "If my spell worked right — and there's no guarantees on that one — he's somewhere in this section of the woods to the northwest of the city."

Max studied the map. He reached over and clicked the mouse to zoom in. "That's a lot of land. How am I supposed to find him in there?"

"How about a little appreciation? You just went from anywhere in North Carolina to a few acres of forest."

He kissed the top of her head. "Sorry. You really did a great job."

"That's more like it."

"Rather than complaining, let me ask this — do you have any suggestions on how to narrow his location any further?"

Her hand quivered as she reached for a glass of water on the coffee table. She gulped it down. "I have one idea, but I don't like it."

"I'm not seeing a lot of choices, so let's hear it."

"He hasn't moved for a long time. A ghost can fixate on something for days if that thing is important enough to them. I don't expect him to leave soon. If he does, he'll have resolved whatever's bugging him, and he can find you with ease. But assuming he'll still be there for several hours, I think you should wait until dark and go out there." Max knew he looked confused, and Sandra picked up on it. "You can see him. His glow will stand out in the dark like a campfire — except ghostly pale and dead."

Max rubbed her shoulders. "That's a really good idea. Why'd you think I wouldn't like it?"

Rolling her neck on the strong feel of his hands, she said, "Oh, y'know — night, alone, ghosts. That's not usually a good combination for us."

"But it's not any ghost. It's Drummond. Nothing to worry about."

Max continued to massage her tense shoulders. Whether he reacted to her words or her physical strain or a combination of both, he did not know, but his fingers started to tap, his mouth dried, and he suddenly had no desire to go out that night.

Chapter 18

AFTER NIGHTFALL, Max drove on Route 67, passing Bethania, and taking Tobaccoville Road. Using his phone's GPS, he turned into the parking lot of the Old Richmond Elementary School — a functional brick building that seemed too large for this remote area. He pulled aside and got out. The tick of his feet on the pavement grew louder with each step.

He headed around back, crossed the sports field, and stopped at the mouth of a hiking trail. Two knee-high posts marked the beginning of the trail and a chain hung between them. Max walked around the chain and headed into the woods. Though probably a trick of his mind, he swore the temperature dropped the moment he could no longer see the road behind.

Using the flashlight app on his phone, he followed the hiking trail deeper amongst the trees. After two minutes, he peered off to the left of the trail — woods and more woods. And also, probably, Drummond.

As he stepped off the trail and walked in the wild, the foliage grew thicker and the trees blotted out any moonlight. The dark encroached, only to be fought back by his single light source. He had to remind himself that he recharged the battery before leaving and double-checked it, too.

He reached the edge of the area Sandra had marked. When he stopped, he thought he heard footsteps behind him also stopping. He scanned the woods in back with his flashlight, but under that light, the forest looked like a gray and pale blue wash — flat and difficult to distinguish where one plant ended or one tree began. And he saw nothing that resembled a person.

A sudden chill rushed over him. He fumbled the phone but kept it from hitting the ground. Woods were one of those places that either had no ghosts in them or overflowed with the dead. It all depended on what had happened there.

If Sandra had come along, she would be able to tell him. Then again, he didn't want to know. A rustle of leaves behind him followed with an icy breeze — he sighed and chuckled at the same time. Nobody followed him. No ghosts had passed through him. Just a cold wind.

"Time to get this done," he said, his voice sounding smaller than he had hoped for. Nonetheless, he touched the screen of his phone, putting the flashlight out. He waited as his eyes adjusted to the night. When he started to see the outline of a tree, he turned slowly in a circle. As Sandra had predicted, he saw a ghostly light off in the distance.

He popped on the flashlight again and walked in the direction of the ghost. Every few minutes, he stopped, turned off the light, waited for his eyes to adjust, and reoriented towards the pale light of Drummond. Seven times Max had to stop. Eventually, he no longer needed the flashlight — Drummond's light let Max see enough.

"You finally showed up," Drummond said with his back to Max.

He floated near an area so dark, Max could hardly make out a tree. Drummond peeked over his shoulder and then touched a tree to his left. A symbol made of swirling lines flashed blue on the bark. Drummond shifted to another tree and lit up another symbol. After two more, the area brightened enough that Max saw they actually stood in a small clearing no bigger than a bedroom.

Drummond hovered near the remnants of a fallen tree. Beyond that, nothing about the area struck Max as notably different from any other part of the forest. Yet Drummond faced that tree with his head bowed and his hat off. One good thing Max noticed — Drummond sounded calm. Sad, but calm.

"If you wanted me out here," Max said, "you could have told me. I would've come."

"I think part of me hoped you wouldn't have to. The fact that you're here means the case has stalled out again. You came looking for my help."

"Well, aren't we full of ourselves?" Max meant it as friendly joke, but Drummond's withdrawn eyes stole any mirth from the air.

"Am I wrong?"

"No. We keep finding routes that lead to nothing, and I have an ugly suspicion about it all."

"And you want to quit."

"You say it like I have a choice. Tell me where to go, what to do, show me what I'm missing, and I'll do it. But the fact is that —"

"The fact is that I didn't tell you the full story." Drummond drifted over the log, gazing down as if he could see through to the heart of the Earth. He slumped even lower. "I knew the moment I shared with you about Detective Cooper, the Dega witch, and that vision of dead children — well, I knew I'd have tell you the rest eventually. I guess I hoped it wouldn't be so soon."

Max knew enough to wait. Drummond continued to glare through the ground. After a few seconds, though, he straightened his back and leveled a determined look at Max.

"I told you that Cooper and I went to a crime scene at a Quaker orphanage."

"Robert Wellman, the headmaster, right?"

"Yeah. Killed by the same witch that inadvertently gave Cooper a vision. That vision warned us that the children were in trouble. Problem was that Cooper never had a vision before. It was over before he even knew what he had seen. He didn't remember much, and what he did remember was vague. Except for the kids. Lined up on the floor, bloody and beaten. He remembered those details all too clearly."

Drummond explained that for several hours he grilled Cooper, trying to extract anything that might point them in the right direction. What did the room look like? Was the floor bare wood or tile or dirt? Was there a rug? Could he smell anything? Hear anything?

"It's a vision," Cooper said. "I only saw things, and I never want to see them again."

Drummond had to make a choice — keep questioning Cooper or sit around and think up some other method of finding the witch. Either one could succeed. Either one could do nothing but waste time. While he had no idea what spell the witch intended to cast that required all these kids nor when the spell needed to be cast, he had no doubt that time was running thin.

He sent Cooper home. The man had been through enough trauma in the last few days, and the repeated questions had only served to push his mind further from the reality he understood. Some people could not handle learning about the world beyond what they knew. Given a few quiet days, Cooper would find a way to dismiss most everything. The things he couldn't fabricate a reason for, he would throw Drummond's way and then do his best to forget about.

Once Cooper left the office, Drummond plunked his feet on his desk and leaned his chair back. And he thought. Every tick of the clock sounded like a hammer strike. Every exhale sounded like a howling wind. He pushed that out of his mind and focused on the witch. What did he know about her?

"Nothing," he said. Floating away from the log and closer to Max, Drummond's eyes flared with his memories. "The crime scenes did not give much either. Maybe in a week they would have, but I knew I didn't have that kind of time. If I was lucky, whatever spell this witch planned would require a full moon. That would give me three days. But there were plenty of other celestial signs that can be used for a spell. As far as I was concerned, I had one night to figure this out. So, knowing that made me desperate, I did a desperate thing. I visited another witch."

Her name was Sally Stroud. She was more than a novice but less than a full-on witch. Like many in the world, she had been raised in a more conventional religion — Methodist, in her case — and she discovered witchcraft late in her life. At fifty-seven, she had been practicing for less than a decade.

But that made her easier to get along with — at least, for Drummond. He never saw a malicious side to her. She once told him that she wanted to understand magic merely to further understand the world. "I don't care about power or influence or any of that. I've got enough money, too."

Drummond paused. He scratched his jaw and made sure he had Max's full attention on this next point. "Sandra used a location spell, didn't she?"

Max didn't like the sound of that. "Yeah. So?"

"She shouldn't start to rely on that. They can be finicky spells. Not always reliable. But all magic, even the little things like a location spell, has a cost. Sally Stroud learned it that night. When I told her what had happened, she wasted no time in setting up a location spell."

Stroud told Drummond it would be difficult to find

another witch, especially one with evil intent. Such a witch would undoubtedly use a ward or spell to hide from prying eyes. But that witch would be stuck when it came to the children. Either she would not shroud them from location spells and such, in which case, Sally could find them easily, or the witch would go to the effort of hiding the children with numerous wards or spells.

"That kind of magic — enough to hide a dozen children — will create a hole in my magical vision," Stroud said. "In other words, I'll be able to guess where she is because there will be a section of the town in which I can't see anything."

Fifty-two minutes passed before she called for Drummond. She said she thought she found them. She wasn't sure, though. Closing her eyes, she said she would push further in.

"Where?" Drummond asked, his fingers clenching.

She swore she could sense them. Glowing.

Placing his ghostly hat back on his pale head, Drummond said, "Max, listen to me. That sweet woman — her eyes burned out. I watched smoke pour from her sockets and flashes of fire. She screamed and fell to the floor dead. I must have stood there for ten minutes, just watching her, like I expected her to get back up and tell me where the kids were hidden. But she never moved again."

"Is that why we're out here?" Max said. "Is she buried here?"

Drummond shook his head slow and deliberate. "I don't know what happened to Sally Stroud's body. I left that night and went back to my office. I grabbed the fake book where I keep my whiskey, and I started drinking. It was over. I had no leads, no way to find those kids, and a witch powerful enough to kill another witch just for looking. Anything I could think of — and to be plain, I couldn't think of anything — it didn't matter. If those kids were alive, they wouldn't be for much longer. It was ugly and terrible, but I drank and reminded myself of the cases I had solved, the good I had done. You can't save everybody, I thought, but at least you tried your best.

"Except I was wrong.

"I had given up, quit because I couldn't think of what to do, when instead, I should have been wracking my brain, going over the case again, searching for any clue, and I should never have stopped until I either succeeded or the police found a bunch of dead bodies."

"I'm sorry," Max said. "And I hear you. That's why I came looking for you. I'm out of ideas, but I hoped you could point me in the right direction."

"You never wanted this case from the start. You came out here hoping that I would tell you it's okay. That you fought the good fight and sometimes you have to lose the battle to win the war. You wanted me to give you an out. But it's not that simple."

Max scowled. "You really think you're responsible for the deaths of those children? You didn't kill them. That witch did. You tried to save them. You can't carry the burden of every death around you. That'll warp your brain. Lead you to self-destruction. If I did that with this case, I wouldn't be able to help any others in the future."

"Told myself pretty much the same thing around my third drink. And maybe, if it all had ended there, maybe I would've woken up the next day hungover but believing that I had done my best and I should move onward. But as I sat at my desk, opening my throat to fiery whiskey, I had a thought — it would have been too hard to move all those kids from the orphanage without being seen or heard. All those kids? Some would have been crying. Some might have even yelled out for help. Herding them out was too cumbersome, too risky."

Max agreed, his mind falling into Drummond's case. "She never left the orphanage, did she?"

Drummond had smacked his leg into his office desk as he stood. Recalling that Cooper had said he couldn't see much in his vision other than the children, Drummond asked himself a crucial question — why? Why couldn't Cooper see anything else? Fear, sure, but for a seasoned cop, fear would have the opposite effect. Cooper should have become hyperaware.

What if he saw nothing because there was nothing to see — because the room was so dark? The only place in that building which would be dark like that — meaning no windows — and also large enough for all the kids had to be the basement. Drummond swept up his coat and hat as he rushed out the door.

Driving from Winston-Salem to Greensboro only took about forty minutes — in 2017. But back in 1939, without a highway system or a car that could hit seventy miles an hour, Drummond had to drive for two hours.

The orphanage, a block of brick and misery, had a cold, empty look that night. Not a light on. Not a sound from inside. Like a sarcophagus — lifeless but not empty.

Drummond picked the lock with ease and entered the welcome lobby. The air smelled strong of cleansing supplies. He guessed the headmaster put the kids to work every day scrubbing, scouring, and sweeping the building to an immaculate state. He wondered who would clean up the headmaster's blood.

With his old .38 in hand, Drummond hustled down one hall and up another in his search for a stairwell. He found it at the end of the second hall. When he opened the door, he heard soft chanting.

As he descended the stairs toward the basement, the chanting grew louder. His heartbeat matched the steady pulse of the witch's voice. The temperature rose with each step down as if he lowered into the depths of Hell. When he finally reached the bottom, he wished for Hell. It would have been a better sight.

The twelve children were all dead. But they no longer rested shoulder-to-shoulder on the ground. Back when Cooper had seen that image, it may have been true. But that time no longer existed. The witch had cast her spell — blood magic requiring the virgin sacrifices of youth and innocence. Powerful stuff.

"I've seen a lot in my time — both when I was alive and after I died," Drummond said, once more drifting toward the log. "Never have I witnessed anything so terrible as I had that night. It wasn't just that the children had been gutted. Or the blood — and there was more blood then I ever experienced. It coated the ground as if a water line had burst and flooded the basement. Everywhere I stepped, I heard the slosh of my shoes in blood. But that was nothing compared to what she had done to their bodies."

"You don't have to go through it all again," Max said, trying to hold back the wobble in his voice. "I get the picture."

"You need to hear it. You need to understand where this all sent me. Because I've seen slaughtered cattle that were treated better."

Drummond stood in that basement, fighting to maintain his sanity while swallowing against the gorge in his throat. The witch had split open the children and gathered their entrails and organs in large bowls. The bodies were then pressed up against the walls, arms and legs spread out, like nightmarish tapestries.

Off to the side, a fire burned on a raised platform. The bowls filled with the children's innards surrounded the platform. In the center, the witch sat on her knees with her arms crossing her chest and her eyes closed. She swayed as she chanted. The stink of burnt meat permeated every inch of the basement.

"I thought the odor came from the children, but I was wrong. The witch, still in a trance of some sort, lowered her hands. I saw twelve, thick crystals embedded in her chest. Each one glowed a soft red."

Max said, "I've never heard of that kind of magic. What was it?"

"I had no idea back then. All I knew was that I could have shot her," Drummond told Max. "I had a sight on her. I could've pulled the trigger and she'd have died before she even heard the gunshot. But the rage swelling inside me wouldn't let it be so easy. She had to suffer. I holstered my .38 and climbed the stairs. At the top, there was a fire ax. I picked it up and as I came back down the stairs, I felt that fire in me blaze strong. I went right after her. That's when I learned what she was doing."

The witch's eyes snapped open. They were filled with a bright, red light. She flicked her wrist and Drummond sailed across the room as if punched by a giant. Back on his feet, he charged again, and once more the witch parried him with barely a motion.

"No way would I get to her by force. So, I did the next best thing — I bluffed. I got up, and this time, instead of running, I stepped as close as I thought she would let me get. Then I looked off to the side and nodded as if I was signaling somebody behind her. Stupid trick, really, but it worked. She turned around, and by the time she spun back on me, angry and ready to kill me, I was already swinging that ax. I buried the blade into her neck. Blood sprayed out to the side, and I yanked it out. She was alive but stunned. I didn't stop. The blade was dull, so I had to hack and hack and hack. Eventually, I chopped her head off.

"It was brutal and horrible, and it was one of the few times I ever had to take a human life. It wasn't over, though. I wouldn't learn this part until later, but now I know that she was trying to do more than gain a lot of power, a lot of strength. She wanted to be immortal. There are some kinds of magic, the rarest kinds, that supposedly tap into the primal forces of all existence. Most witches I've ever talked with about it will say it doesn't exist. That it's nothing more than witch fairy tales. But I know what I saw. In all these decades I've been around, I've never once seen anything like it again."

"You said it wasn't over." Max looked at the log and started to have a bad feeling. "What happened?"

"She had been in the middle of casting her spell. If she had succeeded, according to a trusted source, she would have absorbed the life energy of those kids — when she killed them, she had put that energy into the crystals. Anyway, she would have taken that energy and put it into herself."

"Only that didn't happen."

"No. Yet I could see right away the tragedy I had created. She had no head, no way to speak the proper words, no way to stop what she had started. She was dead but her body refused to die. And the kids ..." Drummond swallowed hard. "The kids were trapped, too."

"Those crystals?"

"Every child had been murdered, yet they could not rest. They couldn't even have the existence I now have as a ghost. They're stuck in those glorified stones, deprived of any solace or rest. Stuck in the unending horror of what had happened to them."

When he faced Max again, there seemed to be tears welling in his eyes. Max figured it was a trick of his ghostly glow in the deep darkness of the woods — after all, ghosts don't have tears — but it sure looked real. Max made a mental note to ask Sandra about the whole tear thing.

Drummond moved in close, reaching out to hold Max's shoulders, and only stopped at the last second. "You've got to believe me. I did everything I could to fix things, but I had to have it all cleaned up before anybody discovered the basement. Once the cops got involved, it would be over. I called Malone."

"Who's that?"

"I never told you about Malone? Oh, he was sort of a mentor to me. When I first got started learning about ghosts and witchcraft and all of it, I self-taught. He found me one day in the occult section of a bookstore. Hey, wipe that astonished look off your face. I can research stuff, too. I just prefer a more hands-on approach to getting information. Anyway, Malone is the one who taught me a lot of the basics. So, I called him in. He took one look and, after he threw up, he said there was nothing we could do. The kind of magic this witch attempted to access is called eternal magic. It's not supposed to exist, and maybe it doesn't. Maybe that's why the whole thing got botched, even if I hadn't killed her.

"Whatever the case, that body with those crystals, those kids, it was stuck forever and there was no breaking it. Worse than that, once word got out, every witch in the area would be trying to get that body. It was powerful stuff, and they would all want it. The Hull family, too. They'd have gone nuts for it, if they ever knew. So, I made sure that never could happen."

Max gestured toward the log. "You brought her out here, didn't you? Buried her under there."

"We did. Put her in a pine box, warded the box, and buried her. Warded all the trees around here, too. Even some of the stones. No spell can find her. No spell can get to her. Nobody can even get close to this spot."

Max recalled how the place looked like a dark copse of trees before Drummond had touched the symbols. "It's cloaked from everybody."

"I'm the only thing that can unlock the symbols, and now I'm the only ghost that can get this close to her. I know those kids aren't at rest, but this was the best I could do for them."

"I'm sorry to hear all that. You know it's not your fault, though."

"Of course it is. Are you listening at all? If I had taken the case seriously from the start, or if I had not given up when I ran out of viable leads, or if I had pushed harder for information from Cooper, or anything like that, the chances are pretty good those kids would have lived a long, healthy life. And if I had still not found them, if I had been too slow getting to that basement, I would have gotten there sooner than I did. I could have stopped those kids from being trapped in that crazy spell. Understand? That's why you can't stop. Not ever. Believe me, you don't want deaths like this on your shoulders."

For a minute, Max said nothing. When he finally spoke, he simply said, "I'm not quitting."

"Good. Then what's our next move?"

"Now who's not listening? I came here to find you because I'm out of leads. Whether you want to hear this part or not, I kind of expected all of this work to go nowhere. I had hoped a lead would pan out, but I'm not surprised."

This pricked Drummond's interest. "Why?"

"Because we've been lied to from the start."

A noise from behind grabbed their attention. Max popped on his phone and spread the light in the direction of the sound. A shadowed figure burst from behind a tree and ran off.

Drummond slapped the symbols on the trees, shrouding the area in darkness. "Get him!" he said as he flew through the pines after the receding figure.

Chapter 19

MAX USED HIS PHONE to light the way as he raced along the uneven terrain. Though his footfalls and breathing filled his ears, he still managed to hear the snapping branches as the man tried to escape. Max peeked off to the right. He glimpsed Drummond's pale light zipping through the dark.

But looking at Drummond meant not looking at the ground. Max's foot snagged a root, taking him down hard. His cheek smacked against a sharp rock, and he felt his warm blood wetting his face.

He clambered back to his feet and searched for any sign of Drummond or the man. Only darkness. Then from behind, he heard Drummond shout in pain.

"For Pete's sake!" Drummond said. "This guy's wearing a ward against me."

Max whirled around and saw the ghost's light. Taking his approach as fast as he dared, Max kept his phone lighting up the way ahead while pausing every few feet to keep oriented on Drummond's glow. But he could tell he moved too slow. If he didn't risk another fall, the man would get away. Drummond could follow him, but since the man had a ward, he most likely had other magic to thwart Drummond in the long run.

Clenching his jaw, Max picked up his pace. He refused to lose another lead. He refused to lose, period.

Keeping his focus on the ground, he sped up, barreling through the brush and weaving around the trees. He tried not to look for Drummond, to trust his own sense of direction and know that his partner would alert him to any major shift. But he still glanced up a few times. The last time he looked, he saw amber lights. They were heading toward the road — apparently, much faster to reach when going in a straight line.

Quit the sarcasm and think!

Shutting off his flashlight, Max pushed onward using the dim streetlights to guide him. Blood trickled into his mouth, coating his tongue with a bitter, coppery taste. Rather than chase after the man, Max angled his approach, hoping to cut off the man's escape.

The man caught sight of Max and angled away like a sailboat tacking for position. Max chanced a glance at the road. He couldn't tell how close they were — too difficult in the half-dark with the streetlights flickering between the trees.

He vaulted over a fallen pine. Sap stuck to his hand. He rubbed his palm against his pants but his mind yelled to stop wasting time — nothing else mattered but catching that man.

"Keep on him, Max," Drummond said. "I got an idea."

He soared about ten feet ahead, then pivoted directly into the man's path. Max understood right away. As Drummond crouched and held his hands over his hat, Max found the strength to run harder.

The man peeked back, saw Max gaining, and pushed on straight for Drummond. Two feet away, the man's ward smacked into Drummond's prone form. Drummond's anguished yell erupted as he fell over, but for the man, it must have been like running into a solid wall.

Max watched as the man flattened into an invisible barrier of his own making. He jolted backwards, flailing his arms as he lurched. His heel twisted on a rock, and Max heard the crash of a body into sticks and leaves.

Shooting forward, Max leaped onto the man. With his

knee locked on the man's chest, Max made a tight fist and struck him hard in the jaw. Twice more he hit the man.

Ignoring the burn in his lungs as he fought to catch his breath, Max pulled back his fist one last time, and said, "Who the hell are you?"

"Get off of me."

"Not until I know who you are and why you're going after the Darden family."

"I'm not going after them. For crying out loud, I'm Enrique Cortez."

Max dropped his fist. "Chelsea Darden's fiancé?" Sitting back, Max allowed Enrique to get up.

Rubbing his jaw, Enrique said, "Yes. Well, no, but sort of. Look, I was assigned to her."

"Assigned?"

"I'm with the Magi group. Mother Hope sent me."

Max's stomach twisted. "Aw, crap."

Chapter 20

SITTING IN THE DINING AREA OF A BOJANGLES — one of the South's many competitors of Kentucky Fried Chicken — Max watched Enrique closely. The left side of the man's face had puffed up from Max's beating, but otherwise, he looked okay. Max had told him they were going to talk, and he asked Enrique to pick a place to sit down, a place he felt safe. He had hoped Enrique would pick some Lexington BBQ or a good Mexican place, but the guy went with fast food chicken. No accounting for taste.

"Look, man," Enrique said, but Max shook his head.

"Wait."

Sitting back in the booth, Max sipped on a cup of water and watched the streets. Enrique tried to speak again, but Max held up one finger and mouthed the word *Wait*. Less than five minutes later, Sandra pulled into the parking lot. Drummond flew from the passenger seat into the dining area.

"I got her up to speed," he said.

Sandra entered. She walked straight to them, sat next to Max, and extended her hand to Enrique. When Enrique hesitated, she snatched her hand back. "That's okay. I don't care for you much either."

He flustered. "I didn't mean —"

"Of course, you did. You work for Mother Hope, after all." To Max, she said, "Let's get this over with. I'd like to get some semblance of sleep tonight."

Max resisted the urge to cup her face in both hands and plant a big, wet kiss on her. "I couldn't agree more," he said. "So, Enrique, don't hold back. If you do, you'll regret it."

Enrique jutted out his chin. "Just because you got lucky and hit me a few times, doesn't mean I'm scared of you."

"Let me give him some brain freeze," Drummond said. "That'll get him talking."

"I never said you were scared of me. But I have no doubt that you are scared of Mother Hope. I have a direct line to her. Now, we can waste more time dancing around like this, but I already know that you are going to talk."

"Really? What makes you think —"

"Because you're here now. Because when I hit you in the woods, you blabbed out about the Magi and Mother Hope. That tells me that you already know who I am. So, stop putting up a front and start talking, or I'll call her right now."

Though ticked off, Enrique raised his hands above the table. "You win. No need to be an ass about it."

Drummond hovered behind the man with his hands at the ready, but Max shook his head gently. "Talk now. Last chance."

"Fine."

Shooting up into the ceiling, Drummond said, "It would've been more fun my way. It would have hurt, but I'm thinking it would've been worth it."

Enrique scooted back. "I've been part of the Magi for about four years now. I was assigned to infiltrate the Darden family, observe and report. Watch over them, if necessary."

"Why?" Max asked.

"I don't know. Really. They never told me."

Enrique reached for a French fry, but Sandra smacked his hand away. "Are you saying that you got engaged to Chelsea as part of a mission? That you faked a first meeting with her, asked her out on a date, seduced her, asked her to marry you — all of that was nothing more than orders? That's disgusting. That woman is a human being. She's got a heart."

Drummond chuckled. "You tell him, doll. I got your back."

Enrique picked up the fry and popped it in his mouth. "This is my purpose. The Magi are here to protect the world from the witches. We stop the abuses of magic that go on all the time. If that means trampling the heart of a woman who, let's be honest here, who has never had a happier time than with me, well, so be it."

Max rested his hand on Sandra's knee — a signal to pull back. However, if Enrique didn't watch his mouth, Sandra would ignore pulling back and deck him. To Enrique, Max said, "Got it. You're trying to stop the Darden family from regaining any of their old witch ways."

"No. I'm only there to report what I see. That's it. Honestly, they're a boring family. Well, Chelsea is. The one you should watch out for is Lane. That girl's dangerous."

"The girl? What about the man who cursed them? Why haven't you done anything about him?"

"I don't know anything about him or his spells."

Sandra pointed a stern finger at him. "How can you call yourself a fiancé, or even just act like one, when you don't even pay attention to the troubles of your soon-to-be wife?"

"She's not going to be my wife." Enrique checked around the dining area — empty except for the staff behind the counter. He leaned closer, rocking on his elbows. "About a week before Aunt Holly died, I was in her private lounge. You seen it? Animal heads stuffed on the walls like some hunter's lodge in the woods."

"Yeah," Max said. "We've seen it."

"I thought I'd take some initiative and see what kind of stuff she had in there. Most times I visited the house, she made it clear I shouldn't go there. But after being engaged, nobody watched me too close when I was at the house."

Before Sandra could comment on how long he had been stringing Chelsea along, Max said, "I'm guessing you found something."

"A journal. She had details on all the kids and —"

Max grabbed the man's shoulder. "Did you read it? The whole thing? What was on the last two pages?"

Enrique shirked off Max's grip. "Dial it back or I'm leaving. I don't care who you think you know. I'm not taking any more abuse from you." He ate some more fries as he spoke. "I didn't get to read the stupid journal. I didn't get anything. I flipped through it, saw the names of the kids, and then Aunt Holly caught me. She had said that she was going downtown to see the family lawyer, but that tricky witch doubled-back and caught me snooping around. We argued. She accused me of being a spy for the Magi. I denied it, but we both knew I was lying. And she threw me out. That was it. Chelsea and the others were outside. None of them heard a thing."

"So, why does Chelsea think you're still engaged?" Sandra asked.

"Because it could be raining outside, but if she wanted a sunny day, then as far as she's concerned it's all sunshine and flowers. I sent her a letter before Aunt Holly died, tried to let her down easy, but man, there's no easy about that. Doesn't matter, though. I knew Chelsea would never accept it. I can't imagine what she tells herself, but I promise you this — we are not getting married."

Max frowned. "You were the same guy spying on me the last few days, right? You peeked through my window. You dressed up in the gray suit and blue tie and assaulted me near the witch hospice."

"Sorry about that. Didn't have a choice. Now that Aunt Holly's dead, I might be able to reinstate myself into the family. I'd make sure the wedding got put off forever, but I might still salvage my assignment."

"But you said —" Max tapped the table and snickered. "Oh, you are in a fix."

Drummond said, "What? What did I miss?"

"Come on, Enrique, tell us the full truth. The Magi don't know any of this, do they? You never told them you got kicked out."

Enrique's lips drew a tight line. Barely opening his mouth, he said, "You say a word and I'll —"

"I say a word, and you'll find out how horrible a person Mother Hope can be." Max derived an ember of satisfaction when he saw Enrique's attitude drop to that of a more humble man. "Back to me — why did you attack me at the hospice? Why did you follow me at all?"

"I was trying to keep an eye on the family, so I saw you there. I knew who you were right away. I followed you because I wanted to find some way to warn you off of this mess without blowing my cover."

"So you beat me?"

Rubbing his puffed jaw, Enrique said, "I guess we're even now. Look, I'm not saying it was the best way to go about it, but I don't know who lives in that hospice — only that there are witches. I couldn't risk anybody recognizing me and telling Chelsea. If any of the Dardens caught me with you or the Magi — I don't want to give that family any reason to discover their deep, inner-witch. Especially Lane."

Sandra said, "Could Lane have killed her aunt?"

"I'd sooner believe Lane killed her own parents. She loved Aunt Holly, and Aunt Holly loved her. Whether the others knew it or not, Lane was being groomed to take over the family and to be the head witch."

Max said, "If you're afraid to be seen with us, why haven't you bolted yet? Why did you choose a public restaurant to talk?"

"You didn't give me much choice." A dark thought appeared to rise on his face but he pushed it away. "To be honest, I'm out of my depth. I've never dealt with anything this big before. For now, though, I don't think they're looking for me. Not out here."

Drummond had his serious face on as he listened intently. He pursed his lips and drifted around the table. "Ask him about the grandmother. She's the one we don't know much about, but if this family is so big on the matriarchal line —"

"What about Grandma Darden?" Max said. "How does she fit in all this?"

"Not much anymore. She was a strong, vibrant lady, but when Holly died, she took it hard. Losing a daughter is tough, I guess. I was never close enough to her to know much. She didn't like me — especially didn't like me for Chelsea. I got that clear. I think she didn't like the idea of a Latino for a son-in-law. Doesn't matter, though. There won't be a wedding, and if there was, she's no longer all there. Her daughter died, and she couldn't take it. Had a stroke or something."

Again, Max caught that dark look on Enrique's face. "There's something you're holding back."

"I'm telling you everything."

"I'm too tired to play another round of guessing games. You know who I am which means you know one of our partners is a ghost. He's itching to freeze part of your body. It's not a pleasant experience."

Drummond flexed his fingers. "Not pleasant for me

either. But if it gets us done here faster."

Looking around, Enrique said, "Come on, man. I'm co-operating. What else do you want to know about? They've got spell books in that huge library, Lane eats macaroni and cheese practically every day, Alan is a prick — what do you want?"

"The hand," Max said. The flash of fear on Enrique's face confirmed that Max had hit the right button. "You know about it, don't you? You're afraid of it."

"You should be too. That thing — I saw it once, by accident. One night, I knocked on Aunt Holly's door to let her know dinner was ready, and the door pushed open. She sat on her bed holding that glass cube, and I could feel the magic coming off of it."

"I didn't feel anything."

"That's sort of the limit of my gift. I'm no good at casting spells or seeing ghosts or anything like that. But I can feel it all. I'm like a Geiger-counter for magic. I'm telling you, that thing scares me more than Lane."

"I'm sorry to hear that because we need it."

"No," Enrique said, and for the first time since they sat down to eat, Max thought the man might try to run off. "You don't really want it, and I won't help you get it. Besides, they'll never let you walk out of the house with that hand. Never. And don't even think about stealing it. The second they notice it missing, they'd raze all of North Carolina to get it back."

Drummond said, "He might be right about that. If that hand meant as much to Aunt Holly as you all seem to think, then we can assume Lane has been taught to think of the hand just as strongly. You steal that thing, and you're basically sentencing somebody to death. Maybe a lot of people. Maybe one of you, if she figures out you're the culprit."

"Relax," Max said to everybody. "I'm not stealing the hand. It was just a thought."

"A stupid thought." Drummond flew back up to the ceiling.

Finishing his sandwich, Max said, "You're still trying to do your mission, so let's get you back on track. I want you to go to the house. Tell Chelsea your letter wasn't true. Tell her you got cold feet. I don't care what you say, but get yourself back in that house. Make nice. You do that, and Mother Hope never has to know about anything that went down tonight."

"What are you gonna do?" Enrique asked.

"Doesn't matter. You do this, and next time we come to the house, you act like you never met us."

"But —"

"Either this or I call Mother Hope. Now, get out of here."

Enrique rushed outside. Max watched as the man pulled out his cellphone. Probably calling a friend to pick him up and take him back to his car.

"So," Sandra said, "I can see the twinkle in your eyes. You've got a plan in mind. Care to tell us what it is?"

"My eyes don't twinkle."

"For me, they do."

"Perhaps."

Drummond forced a cough. "Hey, you two want to get back to the case or am I going to have to haunt this place to stop this disgusting display?"

Max pretended to think it over. "No big plan, yet. But I do have our next move."

"See that? An hour ago you were crying that you had no leads —"

"I was not crying."

"— and now you got a plan to go forward."

"I do. And step one is for you to go follow Enrique Cortez. Make sure he actually does what I asked. It's late, but I suspect he'll go there before the night is over. Tomorrow, meet up with us in Lexington, and let me know what happened."

"You got it. Where in Lexington? What are you two doing?"

"Wouldn't you like to know?" After all the tension of the evening, Max couldn't stop his mouth from a little banter.

Sandra, however, grabbed Max's jaw and turned his head away from Drummond. "Tell me. What are we going to do next?"

Through mushed lips, he said, "We're going to visit Madame Yan."

Chapter 21

MADAME YAN LIVED BENEATH a fading yellow rancher on Rainbow Road off Route 8 in Lexington. The enticing aroma from Speedy's Lexington Barbecue drifted across the homes, the chain link fences, the half-built cars, and the children's toys, and Max thought that if for no other reason than his waistline, it was a good thing he didn't live in this area. They parked on the street and entered the house. Even this late at night, the door was always unlocked.

Inside, they found the living room that had been converted into a waiting room with three couches crowded together. Dim lamps kept a low, shadow-filled light in the room. A woman wearing a black hijab over a white frock walked toward them.

Max snapped his fingers. "It's Cheryl-Lynn, right?"

The woman smiled. In a thick Carolina accent, she said, "Aw, how sweet. You remembered."

"You're hard to forget. Is Madame Yan in? I mean, I know she's in — she never leaves — but is she available?"

"Do you have an appointment?"

"No. See, we need her help with —"

"I'm sorry, Mr. Porter, but Madame Yan only sees people with an appointment. Otherwise, she'd never have time for herself. I mean, everyone who knows her also knows she's always here. Do you realize that people used to come here hours after midnight to talk with her? Kind of like you, right now. Half of them were drunk and the other half desperate. You aren't drunk, are you?"

"No, ma'am."

"The poor woman hardly got any sleep. And how's she gonna cast spells if she can't barely see 'cause her eyelids are half-shut?"

Max wanted to full-shut this conversation. "I understand entirely. Nobody likes having people drop in all the time, but this is —"

"An emergency? Important? Something she would definitely be interested in? I've heard it all. Now, if you want to make an appointment, I'll be happy to get you something set up for as soon as possible. Then you —"

"We must see her."

Sandra stepped in front of Max. "Excuse my husband. He hasn't slept in days."

"Then you understand. It's not a healthy way to run a business."

Walking over to a reception counter that included where the kitchen would be in a normal house, Sandra said, "It's not a healthy way to run a life. So, when is Madame Yan's next available time?"

Cheryl-Lynn scurried behind the counter and consulted a ledger. "Not until Thursday next week."

"I'm afraid that's too far away."

"I can put you on my call list, so if somebody cancels earlier, you'll get the opportunity to take that spot."

Sandra placed a hand on her hip — usually a sign of her anger — only this time, Max could tell it was an act. "You do know who we are, right? I don't mean our names. You know what we do? What we've done?"

The pen in Cheryl-Lynn's hand began to tremble. "I'm aware."

"Then perhaps it's not such a good idea to piss us off."

She looked at her ledger, glanced at the door leading downstairs, and then back at Sandra. "I-I don't know."

"You're kind of stuck now, aren't you?" Sandra said, and

Cheryl-Lynn nodded. "On the one hand, you've got us — people known for destroying a witch or two. On the other hand, you are a good and loyal assistant to Madame Yan — a witch who could destroy you, also. You don't know whose bad side to get on."

"Please, don't do this to me."

"You want to work for a witch, you have to deal with this kind of thing."

"But —"

Sandra turned to Max. "Come on, hon. It's obvious that Madame Yan won't see us. We'll have to take this witch's hand to another. I'm sure somebody else will love to find out how powerful this thing might be."

Before they reached the front door, Cheryl-Lynn said, "Excuse me. Did you say you had a witch's hand?"

"It doesn't matter," Sandra said over her shoulder. "We don't have an appointment."

"Let me see what I can do."

Minutes later, Max and Sandra were escorted into the basement — a spell-casting room decorated like a medieval dungeon. Off to the side, a panel opened up leading to a wide but low-ceiling passage.

"Sorry for the confusion," Cheryl-Lynn said as Max and Sandra ducked their heads. "If you need anything at all, I'll be upstairs."

"Thank you, dear," Sandra said, laying on her own Carolina accent.

Crouching as they moved, Max and Sandra made their way across the dark passage. A single, bare bulb hung in the distance. When they reached the light, they stood before the blue dilapidated door of Madame Yan's real home. They knocked.

"Enter," Madame Yan said in her sing-song voice.

Max opened the door but only a little — he remembered

that the bottom would scrape on the uneven floor and if he pushed too far, it would be like trying to open a wall. Sandra slipped in, and he followed. The room looked much the same as before — normal ceiling height, lots of furniture, and an overall claustrophobic feel.

Books cluttered the furniture. Boxes had been stacked against the walls. Max recalled a stack of birdcages in one corner. They were gone — replaced with a variety of lampshades. Three open boxes of candles — one box of white, one black, one red — sat flush against shelves of porcelain animals. It looked like Noah's ark — lions, bears, elephants, giraffes, monkeys, penguins, and more all cluttered the shelves.

Madame Yan sat atop a mound of books. She wore a black lace dress that fit her heavyset shape well. Max had yet to figure out what part of the world she came from — she had characteristics of practically every major culture and spoke with an equally unidentifiable accent — but he found that mystery rather charming. Her constant grin and frazzled eyes added to her pleasant demeanor, though she had a joint in her hand, so that may have had something to do with it.

"Welcome," she said. "It's been awhile. I started to think I might never see you again. Care for a hit?"

"No, thank you," Max said, wanting to casually lean back but unsure of what would be safe to lean against.

"Your loss. Cheryl-Lynn has a great connection. Gets me some powerful stuff." Pinching the tip of the joint between her fingers to put it out, she said, "You want to talk about the Dardens?"

"You know?"

"Of course, I know." She gave a little shake of her head to Sandra. "How do you put up with him? He doesn't seem too bright."

Sandra elbowed Max. "He's really good in bed."

"That explains it." Madame Yan pulled a rusted sardine tin from a pile of rusted metal and gently placed her joint inside. "Yes, Max, I know about the Dardens. We live in precarious times. Well, all times are precarious to a witch, but recent events — some caused by the two of you — have made life rather unpredictable. It's good for me to know where all the pieces are on the board. Tell me what you know, and I'll try to fill in the gaps."

Max held back. Dealing with a witch, even one as amicable as Madame Yan, always posed dangers. In one breath, she said she knew all about the Dardens, yet in the next, she wanted him to provide information. Plus, and this was most important to remember, nothing from a witch ever came free.

"What do you know about this strange man that put a curse on the house?"

"Oh?" She looked genuinely surprised. "Is that why they've hired you?"

"Can you tell us what the curse is?"

"Dear, it's me. I can tell you lots of things. The question I have is what is it all worth to you?"

"I'd say I already paid you with information you didn't know."

Madame Yan laughed. "Normally, I'd say tough crapola on that one. You gave me something for free there. But, I'm going to be nice — mainly because I'm going to cast a spell to see what's happening there anyway. And I have a feeling doing you a little favor is a big favor to me. Sit tight. Let me go take care of this."

She pushed off the stack of books, toppling three to the floor, and scuttled behind a large dresser. Sandra craned her neck in an attempt to see the witch at work. Max meandered around the room, inspecting one pile of strangeness after another — a box of feathers, a can filled with chewed chewing gum, and an expensive camera from before digital took over.

A minute later, a sharp bang like a firecracker went off. The air smelled of burnt paper. Madame Yan came back with her bangs singed.

"I don't like this at all," she said, fumbling through several piles of books next to two buckets. "Not one bit. Do you know what I found? Of course not, how could you? I cast a spell — easy thing, really — and I found nothing. Which means this man's curse is either extremely powerful, something strong enough to cloak itself, or his spell is weak enough that it blends in with the other spells on the house."

That stopped Max. "Other spells?"

"Sure. A house as old as that is going to have seen a lot of magic. Ah, here." She lifted out a dusty volume and set it atop a diaper changing table. "This is a general history of magic used in the South before the Civil War. That was a strange, dark time for witches and black people alike. And if you happened to be both — life could be short. That happened at the Darden home. Their slaves would figure out that the Dardens had witches in the family, and some of the slaves who practiced magic thought that gave them a common bond. But white people back then did not see black people as human. To them, a negro slave using magic was at best a curiosity and at worst, a threat. The Dardens tended to see it as a threat. Disgusting, if you ask me. If I had the power to do it, I'd see all those plantations destroyed. Maybe leave one to remind and warn people of how horrible we can all be. But live in one? Makes me want to vomit. Here, look."

She turned through several pages of the book. Max had seen photos of lynchings before. He had read copies of slave auction ads and seen the metal collars those men had been forced to wear. But in these pages, he saw photos and drawings of slaves being sacrificed, carved with symbols, and cowering beneath the frightening gaze of witches.

"Not our finest hour." Snapping the book shut, she said, "All those spells back then were not as well-crafted as they are today. Lots of them didn't work. But sometimes, even when a spell fails, residual energy remains. The Darden house is soaked through-and-through with leftover spells."

Max knew the time had come. With Madame Yan caught up in her history lesson, Max hoped she would let slip the answer he sought. "I wonder how that relates to the Kalinski hand we found."

Madame Yan froze. All sound seemed to halt, too. Max couldn't even hear his own heartbeat. Until, finally, she said, "What do you know about that?"

While not the reaction he had wanted, he could work with it. "I know a lot. But as you say, nothing is for free. Care to make an even trade of information?"

Her eyes shifted from Max to Sandra. Then she cackled. "Oh, I like your man. I can see why he's good in bed. He's got big, brass balls." To Max, she said, "You got me with this. But you divulge first. And I want everything you know."

With a nod from Sandra, Max pulled out his cellphone and brought up the pictures he had taken of the hand. Madame Yan pulled back with a gasp when she saw it. Then she approached the phone again, her eyes widening, the tip of her tongue darting along the edge of her lips.

"Holly Darden had the hand in her room," Max said. "Now, I guess Chelsea or Lane will want it. From what I'm hearing, probably Lane." He decided to risk a question, if only to confirm his suspicions. "Do you think this hand is what the man is after?"

As if watching a hypnotist's candle, Madame Yan's eyes never left the photo. "No. Not the hand. It's the ring that's important."

"Your turn. What about the ring?" Max pocketed the phone and noted Madame Yan's dismayed look.

She turned away from Max and picked up the metal sardine tin. After fishing out her joint, she lit it up and inhaled deeply. Pushing aside a box filled with various kinds of salt, she sat on a cushion perched on a stool.

"Are you hungry?" she asked.

"Only for answers." Max wanted to lean heavy on her, make sure she didn't break their deal, but he could see that her stalling came from fear rather than an intent to defraud him. So, he waited.

After another hit off her joint, she pointed to Sandra and then to the box of salt. "Be a dear and put that on the floor." Sandra complied, revealing a second, cushioned stool. "Now, sit next to me."

As Sandra sat, she said, "Are you okay?"

"You know what I think? That you are going to be a very great witch someday. You're a novice, getting your feet wet, but because of what you do with your husband, you keep bumping into powerful magic. That kind of experience forces you to either advance quickly with your skills or perish. I like you. I do. And I hope you advance quickly. So, trust me now — this is not magic you should ever try to work with. This is magic nobody should touch."

"You certainly know how to give a buildup. What's with this ring?"

Madame Yan paused to look at Max and Sandra once more. Max got the feeling she wasn't trying to play the part of dramatic witch but rather that she truly needed to know that they were both paying full attention to her. He saw it in her eyes — what she had to say, she feared saying, so she didn't want to ever repeat it again.

"Have either of you ever heard of *The Malleus Maleficarum?*"

Max had no idea what she was talking about. He glanced at Sandra. She shook her head.

Madame Yan continued, "The title translates to *The Hammer of Witches.* It was written by a Catholic clergyman named Heinrich Kramer and first published in Germany in 1487. It went on to become one of the most widely sold books for hundreds of years. Only the Bible outsold it. And it is, without a doubt, one of the most evil books ever written."

Sandra held Madame Yan's hand. "Go on."

"On the surface, it is an instruction manual for witch hunters. It explains how to spot witches, how to test them, how to apprehend them, torture them, force confessions from them, and kill them. Some consider it a work of pure evil because of all the innocent people throughout history who suffered and died based on its pages. Women burned at the stake who had no interest in witchcraft and had done nothing wrong other than educate themselves or dare contradict a man's view of the world.

"But there's a darker side to this foul book. The real evil lies between its pages. You see, the original book — the master copy — the handwritten manuscript by which the publisher created the book, that document was bound with great forces of malicious magic." She tightened her grip on Sandra's hand. "I'm talking about the kind of powerful magic that would make demons and angels jealous. The kind of thing that would make gods flinch and mortals cringe. To some, to most, there is no greater evil in the form of a book.

"The exact details of what happened have been lost to history, but according to witch lore, there was a fight for the manuscript. In the end, a group of thirteen witches cast a spell to confuse or seduce their enemies — I've heard both versions — so that they could steal the book. They succeeded and disappeared. These witches formed a new coven devoted to protecting the world from the book. They hid it, warded it, cast spells around it, and tasked themselves with guarding it with their lives from any who attempted to take it."

Max hated to interrupt, but he had to ask, "Why didn't they destroy it?"

"It can't be destroyed. Or if it can, nobody has figured out how to do it yet. But it can be used. The magic it contains can be unleashed, wielded as if you held a divine sword. In order to do that, you'd have to open the spellbound locks that surround it. And for that, you'd need a key."

"Like a ring attached to a witch's hand?"

"Oh, yes. That ring is one of the fabled keys."

"I take it that ring would be worth a lot."

"It's beyond value. People will kill for it. Or, in this case, curse an entire family. If that ring is truly one of the key rings, then the Dardens are in great peril. The fact that this man has come after them means word has gotten out about the ring. It won't be long before witches and occultists and others start streaming into North Carolina, each bent on bribing, bullying, or destroying the Dardens."

Sandra said, "But why? What good is a key without the lock to fit it?"

"Because that lock, the original manuscript, is out there. Somewhere. Probably in the archives of a museum. It doesn't matter where. Many witches believe the ring itself holds great power, even without the book. I personally disagree, but that's not a conversation for today."

"Thank you. I'm sure this will help us immensely."

Sandra stood as Max readied to leave. Madame Yan clenched her hand. "You're not listening. This is not magic you want to get near. Either of you. But Sandra, what you have inside you is too precious, too potential, for you to risk messing with this kind of thing. It could destroy you. I don't simply mean kill you. It could rip apart every atom of your soul."

Neither Max nor Sandra spoke another word until they drove off toward Highway 52. Even then, they might have stewed in their thoughts for the entire way home, but Drummond popped up in the back seat. His sudden appearance nearly caused Max to drive off the road.

"I swear we need to get a bell around your neck. Don't do that."

"Got something interesting to tell you," Drummond said with all the exuberance of proud child. "I followed Enrique like you asked and instead of going straight to the Darden house, he detoured to an apartment south of the city. Pretty shabby place sitting on top of a dive bar. He goes into the bedroom and pulls out a suitcase from underneath the bed. I thought he was skipping town, but that wasn't it. The suitcase is filled with wards — each one on a string for a necklace or bracelet. He takes at least eight or so, shoves them in his pocket, and goes to see Chelsea. I'm telling you, he's prepping for a fight."

"Good," Max said. After everything Madame Yan had told them, Max's brain had kicked into overdrive. He had a glimmer of what the truth would be, and if he was right, Enrique might need a lot more than some wards to protect him. "I need to check a few things, make sure I'm seeing all of this right."

"You're not hearing me. Enrique is ready to bust heads. We have to get to the Darden house and either stop him or help him — depends on how you want to play it.

Personally, I think you should confront them with as much as you know but make them think you have the full story. Nine times out of ten, they'll start singing the rest of it for you."

"Maybe, but there are still too many gaps for me to be satisfied. Things we need to understand first. Otherwise, we won't know their lies from the truth."

"If you don't get over there soon, you got a good chance that Enrique's going to blow the whole thing. Doll, back me up."

Sandra gave Drummond a warm smile. "Sorry, but I think Max is right."

"Sure. Side with your husband."

"Enrique's not going to do anything," Max said. "He wants to impress Mother Hope and screwing up his cover won't do that. He'll try to make up with Chelsea."

"But the wards."

"He's protecting himself, not picking a fight. If we go in there now, we'll be blowing everything because we don't understand it all."

Sandra said, "From everything we just learned, I don't even understand why the Dardens hired us in the first place. I think we need to hit the books. Go back over the case and find what we've missed."

Rather than take the exit for Silas Creek Parkway that would lead home, Max headed into the city toward their office. "I agree," he said.

Sandra watched the exit zip by. "I meant in the morning."

Chapter 22

FUELED ON CAFFEINE AND ADRENALINE, Max and Sandra scoured through every detail of the case. They reviewed it in the order of events they had experienced. They reviewed the facts they knew and the things they suspected. They reviewed the various histories they had uncovered. Though nothing jumped out as the key missing detail, Max felt better by seeing all the pieces they did have fit together with some perspective.

Drummond hovered by one of the windows and watched the few late-night drivers roll down the street. "This book, *The Malleus Maleficarum*, you think the Dardens have it?"

Sandra lifted her head from the floor and tried to appear as if she hadn't fallen asleep. "If they had it, they would have used it. And if it's got half the strength that Madame Yan suggested, it would have been like a nuclear bomb going off."

"You mean this could level a city?"

"Not literally. Maybe. I don't know. But amongst the world of witches, I think we all would have felt the shift in energy."

"Then the Dardens are trying to find it. They've got that hand and they need the book."

Max joined Drummond by the window. The city had an empty look to it as if an apocalyptic virus had swept through, taking all the populace and leaving only the buildings behind. But unlike a zombie nightmare scenario, Max could see hints of life and he could sense the slumber of the city. That's what this case felt like to him — a slumbering city waiting for the sun to rise so that it can become active again. Except, he didn't want whatever slumbered in this case to awaken.

"See," Max said, "that's part of what bothers me. Why hire us to deal with this man and his curse when they should have hired us to find the book? They've got the ring and the hand. With the book, they'd have no trouble dealing with this man."

"Why even bother with the hand?" Sandra said. "It's the ring that's important."

The hair on Max's arms stood up. "That's a good question. Why bother showing us the hand at all? And why has nobody taken that ring off the hand?"

Drummond said, "The hand probably has some magic in it."

"Or," Sandra said, "maybe there's a curse on the hand or the ring — something that keeps the two stuck together."

Max tapped his chin as he paced the room. "The hand led us back to Kalinski. Polly Rising, near the end of her life, knew Kalinski and that connection brought us to the Simpson murder. What do those have to do with each other?"

"Don't overthink it," Drummond said as he circled the room with Max. "Lots of people know each other, especially in a group as small and tight-knit as the witches of North Carolina. Rising and Kalinski could have had numerous dealings with each other long before they became roommates."

"Except none of those show up in the history books." That thought stopped Max mid-step. "Why does she show up in the history books at all? She's a minor distraction to the Ann Simpson case."

Sandra got off the floor, her energy uplifted by the others. "I wouldn't call her a minor distraction. She's the one who put the idea of using arsenic in that stupid girl's head."

"That's right. That's more than right." Max clapped his hands and rushed over to his notes. "That's the most important thing. Why did Polly Rising encourage Ann Simpson to murder her husband?"

Sandra looked over his shoulder. "We have to answer the classic question — what did she have to gain?"

"Nothing," Drummond said, moving to the opposite side of the desk. "She left after the murder. Disappeared for a while. From everything you've found, she never got anything out of it. Ann killed her husband, and the fortune teller drifted away."

Max flipped through page after page. "She didn't get any money — nothing significant. She gained a little notoriety."

"As a footnote."

"She had no connection to Alexander Simpson. At least, nothing I could find. Plus, he was too much in love with his wife to cheat on her."

Sandra said, "He loved her so much, he cracked her one in the jaw."

"I'm not saying he was a good man. Just that he doesn't strike me as the kind to cheat. I don't think he had the guts to do it. Plus, he was such a hypochondriac that I think he'd be terrified of contracting some kind of venereal disease."

Drummond said, "Ask this — what happens to Polly by getting rid of both Ann and Alexander? Because that's what happened. Alexander is dead and Ann runs away for a year. Maybe that helps our fortune teller somehow."

"You're right," Sandra said. "What if Polly Rising was playing Ann all along — befriending her, giving fortunes that fed into her interests, working that girl up so that when the time was ripe, a simple word or two pushed Ann to murder? It was a set up. All of it to get rid of both Simpsons."

Max felt the edges of it all connecting. He couldn't see it, but his fingers tingled and he held his breath as he thought. "I'm with you so far. She needs the Simpsons out of the way. Is there somebody else who she couldn't approach while they were around? Maybe Ann's old lover?"

Max saw realization break on Sandra's face. She said, "What if it was the house that she wanted?"

"But after the Simpsons were done with, Polly didn't buy the house," Drummond said.

"She didn't need to," Max said. "She only needed to gain access to the house." This was it. He knew it. All the players straight through to Chelsea and Lane fit this scenario. "I know what happened. And now, Drummond's right. It's time to go visit the Dardens."

"Honey," Sandra said, "it's four in the morning."

He checked the clock on his computer. "Oh. In that case, Drummond and I need to rest up — well, whatever ghosts do instead of rest. Sandra, I need you to prepare a special spell. If you can't do it, if it's too difficult, you have to let me know. We'll go see Madame Yan or we can—"

"I'll get it to work. Give me the details."

As Max explained his plan, a thought both dark and bright popped in his head. *When the sun rises, this ends.*

Chapter 23

THE DAWN PRESSED OUT GOLDEN RAYS across the Darden plantation. Max, Sandra, and Drummond stood before the pillared entrance with the warm sun cutting across the fields. Max walked back toward the car, trying to clear his mind, to get his brain to calm down.

That morning as they had prepared to leave, Max's mother clumped downstairs. "Where are you off to?" she asked.

"We've got to meet with our clients," Max said, reviewing the notes he had made.

"So early?"

"Yes, Mom. We're trying to wrap up the case."

"Well, let me join you. I'll get the boys and —"

"No. This is just me and Sandra. I don't want you or those boys near that house."

"Why not?"

"It's dangerous."

"Then why are you going?"

The conversation never got any easier. PB and J were both good at knowing how they fit in the agency. They were family, but they weren't expected to be working all the time. In fact, Max had made it an unspoken policy that if the situation looked dangerous, those boys would not be involved. He felt the same about his mother, yet she did not see it the same.

Driving to the Dardens, Sandra expressed concern over the spell she had concocted. "Once it goes off, everybody will know. Won't that put you in a tough spot?"

"I can handle it," he said. "Drummond will be there and I suspect there will be enough shouting and confusion that they might not notice what you're up to."

Finally, when they arrived and Max saw the blue BMW by the side of the house, the weight of the plan hit Max hard. Drummond flew through the walls to check that the family had assembled — including Enrique Cortez — while Max and Sandra stood outside. Waiting.

Sandra came up behind him and stroked his back. "Hon?"

"A case of the jitters, I guess." He felt like an actor waiting in the wings, praying that nobody had changed the show on him.

She kissed his cheek. "You'll be fine. Besides, this is your chance to tap into your inner-Poirot."

The corner of his mouth lifted. "Now I'm wishing I read more Agatha Christie. You sure you can do this?"

"Oh, my spell is going to go off. Whether it will work how we planned, well, that's another matter. But something will happen."

"Okay, then. Let's go."

Hand in hand they strolled back up to the front door and rang the bell. Chelsea opened the door but offered no smile. "Everyone's here. I put them in the living room."

As Max walked in, he glanced up. An ancient symbol had been drawn in the doorway. Good. Another piece confirmed.

He followed Chelsea into the living room. Grandma Darden sat in her wheelchair near the back. Alan stood behind her, his balding head shinier than usual. Looking perturbed at the disruption of her day, Lane had curled her feet under her on one end of the couch. Enrique sat on the other end of the couch with one leg crossing the other. Chelsea pulled over a wooden chair and set it as far away from Enrique as she could without looking rude to the rest of the family.

"Where's your wife?" she asked after she sat.

"She'll be here in a minute," Max said. "For now, I want to explain to you everything that's been going on because some of you are misinformed while others of you are ill-intentioned."

"Are you really going to begin this morning by insulting us?" Alan said, his meager chest puffing.

Drummond descended through the ceiling and winked at Max. "She's all set. Said she needs at least ten minutes to get the spell to work — if it works. Her words, not mine."

Max nodded as he stepped forward. "I have been involved with many cases that touch upon things like witchcraft, and it has been my experience that when dealing with witches, one must always be on the lookout for deceit. It's not that witches are evil people — in fact, most of the time, they are trying to do what they think is best. I suspect that repeated use of magic — constantly taking the natural state of things and altering it — starts to alter the natural state of the mind as well." He looked up at Drummond. "I really believe that."

"I know, pal. But you and I are watching Sandra close. We'll know long before it ever reaches that point, and I promise you this — if it ever gets too bad, we'll put a stop to it."

"This change in a person's mind can take many forms but the most common that I have come across is lying. Always lying. A witch that has been around for a hundred years, casting spells on a daily basis, will lie about what she had for breakfast. She'll lie about her name. She'll lie about the weather or even what color socks she's wearing. In the case of this family, everything I've come across has been one lie after another."

Chelsea glanced at Enrique and turned away. She dabbed at her eyes. "Mr. Porter," she said with a surprisingly firm voice, "we have not been lying to you. The man that cursed us —"

"Ah, yes, the man who cursed you." Max raised one finger as if making a thoughtful point and moved towards her. "Let's begin there with Lie #1 — there is no man. And Lie #2 — there is no curse."

"That's ridiculous."

"Did you ever see the man? You told me that you were asleep when he came."

Chelsea paused. "Yes, but I heard him arguing with Alan, and when I came down the stairs, he ran off to his car and drove away. I saw him do that. So there was a man."

"I apologize. I misspoke. You see, there was a man, but not the one you think. And there was a curse, but not the one you think."

"I'm confused."

"So was I. But it is all becoming quite clear. Let's begin with the curse. This curse is quite unusual. It bans the four of you from leaving this house yet has no effect on any other. I've had no trouble getting in. My wife has had no trouble getting in. Your lawyer, Mr. Mane, he has come and gone without issue. You said that you've had food delivered. Even my partner, with his unique situation, has had no trouble coming in or leaving.

"Now, a curse which could be so selective over such a large home would have to be strong. In other words, it couldn't be as simple as the single, scrawled symbol on a pillar outside which you described. In fact, I've looked at the pillars out front, and there are no symbols on them at all. So, I then had some of my associates walk the entire perimeter of this property."

Lane snorted. "That must've been a hell of a hike."

"It certainly was. And do you know what they found?"

Alan wrinkled his nose. In a monotone, he said, "Oh, please, tell us. We're enjoying this so much."

"They found nothing. Not a single thing. I have personally seen a similar type of spell used to prevent anybody from coming in or out of a specific location. This was a small area in the woods no larger than this living room. And the spell did not protect the actual area but rather a single point within the area. But every tree surrounding that point bore an archaic symbol on the bark to aid in casting the spell and to keep it going. Even some of the rocks had symbols. Yet for a spell so massively selective and powerful that it could keep the four of you locked in this house, we find not one single symbol."

Chelsea's gaze drifted around the room. "What does that mean?"

"It means that there is no spell, no curse, on this house preventing you from leaving. You can go anytime you wish."

"But I saw Alan. He fell over in pain when he tried to leave."

Alan rushed over to Chelsea. "I'm sorry, Sis. I was only trying to protect you."

"From what?"

Savoring this perfect moment in his speech, Max wagged his finger in the air and said a bit too dramatically, "Not from *what* but from *whom* — isn't that right, Alan?"

Alan came close to spoiling Max's enjoyment, but the seriousness of the situation returned his attention to Chelsea. "It was Enrique, Sis. He came that day — not some man trying to hurt us — just a man who I knew would hurt you. He's going to break your heart."

Pressing back a tear from her eye, Chelsea said, "He already has."

Max went on, "You see, Chelsea, Enrique was not going to marry you. Not then. He'd already called it off, but you did not seem to want to accept it. He had come to the house to make one final attempt at getting through to you. But Alan stood in his way. For you, Alan made up the story of the man."

Her hand dropped to her cheek as if she had been slapped. "You lied to me for weeks? Kept me here for that?"

"Allow me to continue," Max said. "The plan was not to leave you in the house for so long. It was only meant to be a few days, enough time for you to calm down. Unfortunately, you called me and that started to make things difficult. But before we get into the reasons behind that, we still have one other issue to address. We now understand the lie of the man and that of the curse — except that lie of the curse is only a half-lie. Because there is a curse on this house, but it does not prevent you all from leaving. It only effects one person here — Grandma Darden.

"I saw the mark on your front door. I'm sure when I inspect the other entrances and exits to the house, I will find more. Grandma Darden's sudden stroke was no accident. It is the effect of the curse, the one she is trapped in right now, the one that stops her from talking."

"Mr. Porter, everything out of your mouth is shocking me. I don't understand. Why would anybody want to hurt Grandma Darden?"

In what he hoped to be an impressive move, Max whirled on Chelsea. "That is an excellent question. It brings us to the heart of the matter. We've dispensed with the myth of the man and the curse, but why is any of this happening? Why go to all these lengths? For an answer, we have to go into the history of your family and what your purpose is in the world of magic and witchcraft."

From the ceiling, Drummond clapped his hands. "You're doing a great job. I can count on one hand the number of times I got to solve a case this way. Enjoy every minute of it, pal." Max put his hands behind his back and tapped the face of his watch. Drummond answered, "I got it. I'll check on her and see how much more time she needs."

Using a thoughtful pause, Max made eye contact with each sibling, ending with Chelsea. "Your family has a singular, unique position when it comes to magic. I had never considered the possibility before this case, though the evidence was right in front of my nose the whole time. You see, many witches are generalists — they can cast any spell. They have to work hard at it, learn over decades, practice hundreds of hours, and only a few will ever become truly adept at it. But others are specialized.

"Take me, for example. I'm no witch, and I can't cast a spell with any ease or consistency. I'm not good at it. But I can see a ghost — one ghost only. I can see him, interact with him, and work with him quite successfully. I've also met a man who cannot cast a spell at all and must rely on magic created by others, but his true specialized skill is that he can detect magic, feel it when it is near. You see? Specialized. That is also a part of your family — a very specialized ability. Something that would have been easier to understand had the last two pages of Aunt Holly's journal not been destroyed."

With a flippant toss of her hand, Lane said, "Now we're specialized witches? You make as much sense as Alan does when he's drunk — which is most of the time."

Letting his voice take a heavier tone, Max said, "Oh, you are specialized. Very much so. All this talk by Aunt Holly of reviving witchcraft in the family meant a lot. It meant everything. Because your family's place is one of protecting the world's witches. You don't possess a generalist's ability, but the special power you have is stronger than most witches dream of having. It is a power that has been with your family generation after generation stretching all the way back to your origins in Germany. Grandma Darden knows all about it. She's the one who passed down the knowledge to Aunt Holly. And Aunt Holly was grooming you, Lane, to take over. Wasn't she?"

Lane crossed her arms and huffed. "So? She showed me a few magic tricks."

"Quite a bit more than a few tricks. This is the other information that I missed from those torn out pages. Aunt Holly had decided to take things a step further. She wanted to do as Grandma Darden had taught her — to continue the family tradition of protecting witches — but she also saw an opportunity to do so by controlling the witches."

Chelsea slapped her hands on her knees. "Mr. Porter, I've about had enough. What you're saying is making no sense to me at all."

Max knew he had been working in a circuitous route and hoped he didn't sound like too much of an idiot, but he had to give Sandra every possible second he could create. Thankfully, Drummond's head poked out of the ceiling.

"Time to wrap it up," the ghost said.

"My apologies, Ms. Chelsea. I was trying to be sensitive towards everybody's feelings and to your memory of your dear, departed Aunt. But allow me to be blunt.

"For generations, your family has been tasked with the unique job of protecting witches from a book. *The Malleus Maleficarum — The Hammer of Witches*. Your ancestors formed the first coven that took possession of this book and hid it. Somewhere in this house is the original manuscript and all the evil magic that rests within it. It is not something that can be destroyed. Whether by choice or whether assigned the duty, your family took on the job of learning, practicing, and excelling in all the magic necessary to prevent others from getting to it.

"But then along came a fortune teller. Polly Rising. If we think of the book as a door into massive power, then the spells the Dardens put upon the book are the lock. Polly discovered the key. It was hidden somewhere in an empty house in Fayetteville, North Carolina. But before she could get hold of this key, a young couple bought the house and moved in. It took Polly a few years, but she eventually manipulated the young wife into murdering her husband. With the husband gone and the wife surely to be locked up — though as it turned out, the wife fled town — Polly Rising had access to the house for a short time. Under cover of darkness, she broke in and found what she sought — a ring. Afterwards, she ran away.

"All she needed now was the book. But while all of us in this room know of the Darden family's job, most witches don't even know if the original manuscript to the book still exists — let alone if it truly holds the power claimed. But Polly had the ring, so she felt confident the tales about the book must be true, too.

"Somewhere along the line, as she neared the end of her life, she met up with Danica Kalinski. It's unclear exactly how things worked out between them, but it didn't go well. In the end, we know that Polly no longer had the ring, and that Miss Kalinski eventually lost her hand with the ring stuck on her finger."

Chelsea's stunned face turned straight to Max. "The hand in the glass cube?"

"The day your Aunt Holly brought that home, she was ecstatic. She thought she could use that ring to access the book and gain unimaginable power."

With a pompous gait, Alan strutted up to Max. "This is absurd. If this ring could open this book that we supposedly have, why wouldn't we have done it already? Why didn't Aunt Holly open the book and make us all super-powerful beyond imagination? It's ridiculous. This is nothing but the sick, twisted, malicious fantasy of a two-bit detective who is upset because he got paid to handle a fake case."

Max swallowed down the rebuttal he wanted to make. This wasn't about scoring points. Instead, he let Alan's words hang in the air until it felt uncomfortable. Then, he said, "Insults aside, you bring up a good question. Why didn't Aunt Holly open the book? The reason is sitting right here — Grandma Darden.

"She is a true believer. She takes the oath your family has made to protect the world from *The Malleus Maleficarum* quite seriously. To her core. Aunt Holly knew this. That's why she hid the hand in her bedroom closet. And she waited. At some point, Grandma Darden would die, at which time Aunt Holly would be the senior witch in the family and would be free to use the ring."

Staring at her phone, Lane giggled. "You're telling us that the reason Aunt Holly didn't grab hold of huge amounts of power was to spare Grandma Darden's feelings?"

"That would seem silly. So, no. The reason she had to wait is because the ring is not an instant key. You can't simply touch the book with it and the power is yours. Magic this strong is never that simple. It takes time to cast the spell and requires a large casting circle. Grandma Darden would clearly discover this happening and put a stop to it. In fact, Grandma Darden would curse Aunt Holly, and if that didn't work, I think her belief in her oath would lead her to kill Aunt Holly."

Lane whipped her head towards the family. "Are you saying Grandma Darden killed Aunt Holly?"

Max walked around the edge of the room towards Grandma Darden. "I am saying that your beloved grandmother *would have* killed Aunt Holly were it necessary. However, we know that Aunt Holly died of natural causes. That was unexpected and inconvenient — especially to those in the family who wanted to share in the power of that book."

Alan shook his head. "Who are you talking about now? You're not about to spring an illegitimate brother or sister on us, are you?"

"I'm talking about Lane. Your sister never knew your parents. Aunt Holly is the only mother she ever connected with. She has been raised and trained by Aunt Holly. Lane loved Aunt Holly. Worshiped her, really. And Aunt Holly indoctrinated Lane to believe that opening the book, unlocking that power, is your true birthright. That's what this is all about.

"I suspect the moment Aunt Holly died, Grandma Darden saw what would happen. Maybe she even caught Lane in Aunt Holly's bedroom. Perhaps Lane held the glass cube with the hand and ring. That's when the real curse was put on this house.

"Realizing the danger Lane posed, Grandma Darden had a problem. She could have mustered the courage to kill Aunt Holly, her own daughter, if it meant fulfilling her oath. But her granddaughter? A girl still in her teens who really couldn't be responsible for the way she had been raised? She refused. Instead, she sacrificed herself. Took herself out of the equation. She put a curse on the house to stop anybody from being able to learn the secrets she held in her old mind."

Lane laughed. "You're babbling like a fool. You sound

moronic. This whole family meeting is a waste. Can I please go chat with my friends?"

In the coldest voice Max had ever heard from her, Chelsea said, "Young lady, you stay seated. I want to hear the rest of this."

"Not clear enough? It's simple," Max said. "At some point, Grandma Darden began to suspect Aunt Holly's real motives. So, in addition to the various spells that exist to protect the book from being used, your grandmother cast more. By cursing herself, she muted her ability to tell you what those spells are. You could torture her forever, and even if she broke and desperately wanted to tell you, the curse prevents her. It also blocks anybody attempting to get into her head through magic. All of that meant that Lane could not just grab the ring and open the book.

"She's been taking her time. Acting like a teenager and spending all available moments online. But she's not chatting with friends or looking at cute kitten videos. She's scouring every craft site there is to find the answers to breaking that curse. Chelsea, when Alan argued with Enrique and created his little lie to cover it all up, Lane utilized that against you to make sure that you and Grandma Darden were kept under complete control. She knew Alan wouldn't care about any of this. Witchcraft and the family legacy don't interest him. Why should it? It had been made clear to him that only the women in the family mattered.

"The only real problem was me. Isn't that right, Lane? You didn't expect Chelsea to do anything about the fake curse except cower in her bedroom until you told her it was safe. And that might have worked. But the days went by and you couldn't break the spells on the book. After a while, Chelsea surprised you by taking some initiative. She called me.

"You couldn't really turn us away because you would end up having to admit there was a fake curse on your family. So, you hoped I would spend my time spinning my wheels, not being able to find anything, and by the time we figured out what was going on — *if* we ever figured it out — it wouldn't matter anymore. Is that clear enough for you?"

An unsettling quiet descended on the room as all eyes turned towards Lane. She sat still and poised as if interviewing for a secretary position in the 1960s. When she finally moved to turn her head, all the teenage attitude had disappeared. In its place, Max saw the calculating maturity of a seasoned politician.

Unable to handle the quiet, Chelsea blurted out, "Aren't you going to defend yourself? He's accusing you of manipulating me and Alan and forcing Grandma Darden to curse herself and he's saying that you —"

"Why are you so stupid?" Lane said, causing Chelsea to stammer into silence. "I've been sitting here the entire time. I've heard every word."

Trying to maintain some order, Max said, "I'm glad you're not denying any of it."

"What would be the point?"

"I agree."

"But in your haste to paint me as the villain, you've left out an important fact."

"That's right," Chelsea said. "I knew there would be a reason. Please, explain to Mr. Porter why he's wrong."

Lane stood. Before she spoke any further, she took the time to level a disgusted gaze at Chelsea. Then, in a voice that grew harsher with each syllable, she said, "Should I do that, Mr. Porter?" She slithered towards him. "Should I explain why you're wrong? Or should I show you all how strong I really am? Should I make it clear to you that I am going to take what rightfully belongs to the Darden women? Do I need to explain that I have no problem killing all of you, if you stand in my way?"

Chapter 24

OVER THE YEARS working on these paranormal cases, Max had learned that he could count on only a few things. He could count on Sandra and Drummond. He could count on the rest of his team. And he could count on the fact that nothing would ever go according to plan. So it came as no surprise when Drummond dropped in front of him and said, "Got a little hiccup."

Max could not have a conversation with Drummond, so a raised eyebrow had to suffice.

"Oh, right. Apparently, Sandra's spell isn't working. It's close though. She's on the internet trying to figure out where she made a mistake. You need to stall for a few minutes more."

"Are you crazy?" Max said.

Lane grabbed the dancing bear figurine from the coffee table and threw it right over Max's head. It smashed into the flatscreen television, leaving behind two sharp cracks. "Don't ever call a witch crazy. Too many of our kind were locked up under that false term."

With fast, shallow breaths, Chelsea said, "You just broke a five hundred dollar figurine and a fifteen hundred dollar television. I think that qualifies as crazy."

"Oh, my dear sister. You could have had so much, if you only had been strong enough to take it. But don't worry. Stay with me and I'll teach you everything you should have learned."

Lane put out her hand, and Max saw sincerity in her young eyes. Of course — she had been raised to be power-hungry, but also to value her family. The women in the family, at least.

Enrique rose from the couch, bent and slow as if a heavy chain held him by the neck. "Lane, put your hand down. Chelsea does not belong to you."

"Look who suddenly has guts." Lane lowered her hand as she approached Enrique. "You better watch it. I'm not bluffing when I say I'm strong."

"I think you are bluffing. For now. Max wasn't lying when he said people like you specialize in spells. I can see the truth. You're not so strong. You have no spell that will kill us." Enrique glanced down at Chelsea with a glisten in his eyes that had to be an apology. He turned back to Lane. "What good will all that power you gain be, if you can't leave this house?"

Lane grinned. "Back to that? Did you not listen? It was a lie. We faked it. There is no curse keeping us here."

"Not yet."

"Now who's bluffing? You can't cast spells. You've got no power to curse this house."

Enrique thrust his hand into his pocket and pulled out seven wards on seven strings. "These do."

Drummond whipped his head around. "Don't let him do that or I'll —"

Uttering a deep shout, Enrique threw the wards into the air. As they rose toward the ceiling, he dropped his head and mumbled a phrase that Max could not make out clearly. At the height of ascent, that moment when the wards hovered in the air before gravity brought them back down, they each snapped in two. A bright light filled the room. Chelsea cried out as everybody covered their eyes. Max heard Drummond yell, and as the light faded, he saw that his partner had disappeared.

"What did you do?" Lane said.

Enrique sat on the couch with his head up and a cocky grin. "Try getting out of here now."

Lane dashed out of the room and threw open the front door. She walked straight ahead at the open doorway and slammed into an unseen wall. Max never liked the Magi, but he had to hand it to this man. Enrique had just bought them all a few more minutes.

From the corner of his eye, Max caught movement by the window. Snatching a peek, he spied Drummond — stuck outside. The ward must have thrown out any ghosts in the house.

Lane grabbed the figurines on the mail table and threw them at the door. They shattered in the air. "Lower this ward." She stomped back to the living room, right up to Enrique. "Lower this ward now, or I will kill you."

He crossed his legs. "If you don't have the magic to lower a simple ward like that, then you don't have the magic to kill me, either."

"Who needs magic?"

She raised her arm. Max looked out the living room, across the foyer, and saw the empty mail table by the front door. He spun back but it was too late. In Lane's hand, she wielded the letter opener.

Chelsea shrieked as she watched her sister bury the sharp blade into Enrique's neck. Blood spurted into the air. Enrique sat stiff with eyes wide in shock. A soft wheeze gurgled through the blood around the letter opener sticking out of his skin.

Calm and cold, Lane faced the rest of the room. A crimson line of Enrique's blood marred the left side of her face like a scar across her eye and cheek. With careful, controlled grace, she walked out of the room.

Chelsea launched over the couch. She picked up Enrique's lifeless hand and held it to her heart. Stroking his face, she cried. "Honey? Sweetheart? My love? Wake up. Look at me." Her words drifted in and out of being audible like waves on a quiet afternoon. "I'm sorry about the wedding, about our fights. I forgive you. I love you. I can wait to get married. It's okay."

Lane returned carrying a brass bowl. Max's stomach dropped. He had seen bowls like that before. They were used to collect blood for casting dark spells. Back then, he had been handcuffed to a basement pipe and unable to stop the proceedings. Not this time.

"Out of my way," Lane said, kneeing Chelsea aside.

Max darted forward, but after only two steps, he froze. Alan had pulled out a 9mm handgun and pointed it in Max's direction. "I'd like you to step back."

Chelsea let loose another bawling cry. "Alan? You, too?"

Chapter 25

ALAN SNEERED AT CHELSEA as he motioned for her to stand next to Max. "You act so surprised which is enough to make me shoot you right now."

Max offered a knowing nod. "You're right. I should have seen it."

"I don't care about you. Why should you have had any idea what goes on in this house? But Chelsea — you sit here day after day thinking so little of me. *Oh, that poor Alan. He's so lazy. Won't he ever do anything?* And all that time, I watched and listened. I knew Lane would take over this family, and I knew Aunt Holly had a chance to make us all powerful."

With the brass bowl close to full, Lane walked into the foyer. "Come on, Alan. Bring them in here."

Gesturing with the handgun, Alan said, "You heard her. Go on."

Max's brain scrambled for an idea, any idea, of what to do. With Drummond locked out of the house and Sandra's spell failing, he had no recourse but to handle it alone. Except he couldn't outrun a bullet. Which left him only with his mouth.

"You know this won't end well for you," Max said. "Witchcraft is all about women."

"Don't even try to act like you know anything."

"That's why you were cut out of the Will. Actually, the phrase *cut out* implies you were once *in* the Will, and we all know that isn't true. If Aunt Holly didn't see it fit to give you even a little bit of money, not even an allowance, what makes you think Lane is going to do any different? She was Aunt Holly's prized pet."

Max had no clue what all his verbal baiting would accomplish, but it made him feel better. If he had any luck, he might be able to distract Alan or change the way he thinks or create a lucky break.

Lane set the bowl on the floor near the stairs. To Max, she said, "You can keep talking, if you want. You won't do any good, though. My brother has always known how to play the odds. Anybody with half-a-brain can see that odds favor me most."

Screaming, Chelsea said, "You didn't have to kill him!" She fell to her knees, heaving sobs into her arms.

With her meanest smile, Lane said, "You're right." She crossed the foyer, reached down, and lifted the edge of the large, round rug situated underneath the stained-glass dome. Walking backwards, she pulled the rug away, revealing a circle made of mosaic tiles embedded in the floor. Symbols lined two concentric inner-circles, and words in dead languages forgotten by all except those who know witchcraft had been carefully written along the entire outer-edge.

"Under our feet the whole time," Max said, the scope of his defeat increasing with every moment. Drummond had been right all along. If Max hadn't wasted time trying to avoid the case, if he hadn't given up with each dead end, this might not have happened. But every step that he tried to get away from the case only served to give Lane more time to break the spells protecting the book.

This was all his fault.

He had known it all along, too. Deep inside. That always seemed to be the truth of things. No matter what the issue, he generally knew what the right thing to do was — except he often resisted. Worse, that resistance usually required more energy than facing whatever truth he wanted to avoid.

Lane pulled her hair back and tied it into a ponytail. "Keep them here. I'll be right back."

As she walked down the hall, Alan shifted his position to the side a few feet. "I know how this whole thing looks, but you ought to trust me."

"You've got a gun on me. Why should I trust you for anything?" Max said.

"Not you." Keeping his handgun at the ready, Alan squatted to Chelsea's level. "Sis, listen to me. That guy was no good for you. Everybody could see that. Aunt Holly, Grandma Darden, Lane, and I only want what's best for you and for the family. Enrique had only his own interests at heart. Why do you think I was fighting with him that day?"

"She killed him!" Chelsea's outburst choke back into silent sobs.

"She shouldn't have done that. Lane's got a lot of strength, but she still acts out like a teenager. That's not an excuse, but I'm sure she'll feel sorry and apologize after things calm down."

Chelsea's glare quieted Alan. He stood and reasserted his stance near Max. "You move wrong, and I'll shoot."

"I'm not going to try anything."

When Lane walked back up the hall, she carried a short knife and a basting brush from the kitchen. She picked up the bowl and walked into the center of the circle. Lowering to her knees, she bowed her head and closed her eyes.

Something felt off. It might have been the losing position Max found himself in, but no — he could tell something had gone wrong for Lane and Alan. Observing them closer, he picked up on part of it — Lane was praying. As far as Max knew — and admittedly, he had a lot to learn about witchcraft — no spell required prayers.

Witches didn't believe in deities — not, at least, as a source for magic. So, why was Lane praying?

"Oh, no," Max whispered. To Alan, he said, "She failed."

"Shut up." Alan gestured with the handgun.

"You don't get it. She couldn't figure out how to safely break Grandma Darden's curse or any of the magic protecting the book."

Lane opened her eyes. She had lost the calmness from earlier. Max could see her trying to summon the courage for what would come next.

"Look at her," he said. "She can't win the way she had planned, so she's going to break through to that book with sheer force."

Alan's confidence wavered. "What does that mean? She's going dig through the floor."

"No," Lane said, standing up. She dipped the brush into the bowl of blood and painted a straight line on the floor. "We could dig for ages and we'd never get what we want."

"But we're here, so you have some plan to get the book, right?"

She painted another straight line connecting with the first, and Max's pulse quickened. He knew what she would do and it might be strong enough to work. She said, "Aunt Holly taught me about the protection wards and the various curses we've used on the book. To break them requires great skill and power, far more than I ever had. I was cocky to think I could figure it out in only a few weeks."

"Then what are we doing? You said we'd share all this power. That we'd be able to take over."

"We will." She painted a third line connecting with the other two. "You see this?"

Alan looked at the blood on the floor. "It's a triangle. So what?"

She returned to her knees and placed the knife in front of her. "Go on, Mr. Porter. You had so much fun explaining everything earlier. Tell my dear brother what I'm going to do."

Come on, Sandra. Save my butt.

Alan licked his lips and bounced his free hand against his side. "Tell me. She told you to tell me, so do it already."

With a resigned nod, Max said, "Your sister couldn't come up with an elegant or practical solution, so she's going to try to bully her way through. She's going to use the darkest, strongest, worst forms of magic. She's going to war with the spells that your family has set down for generations. That's what the triangle is for. A casting circle represents unity, the oneness of all. It helps bind the magic between the caster and the surrounding elements. But a triangle is like a jagged knife trying to cut through that unity and force it to obey the caster's commands."

"That's not so bad. She's good at this kind of thing. I've seen her. She can pull this off."

"No, she can't. And she knows it. That's why she brought the knife."

Alan's hand went to his throat. "She's going to kill me, isn't she? She's going to use my blood like she's using Enrique's."

"Relax, Alan." Max didn't like the way Alan's finger kept grazing the trigger. "The knife isn't for you."

Lane stood and held the knife between both hands as if clasped in prayer. "In the name of all Dardens who have come before me, those witches that sacrificed their lives to protect our power, I call upon you to aid me, last in the Darden line, to unleash that which we have kept hidden for so long. To you, I give my sacrifice."

Max wanted to look away. He knew he would be seeing Lane and that knife for years to come in his nightmares, but he had to stay alert. He had to be ready should an opportunity for escape present itself.

Chelsea's mournful moan found its match in Alan's horrified gasps. Max stayed silent.

With a sudden motion, Lane jabbed the knife into her left eye socket. Though she screamed, she did not falter. Constant motion and a vicious yet steady hand cut out her eye. Tears of blood streamed down her cheek but she continued to cut. And scream. Her screams haunted the halls and rooms, echoing throughout the house like the centuries of horror that had occurred on this land. When she finished, she bowed her head and let her sacrifice fall to the floor.

Time had run out. If there had been a chance to make a move, Max knew he had missed it. The spell had been drawn; the sacrifice had been made. Max could think of only one desperate move — lunge across the room and hope to rub open part of the triangle, breaking the spell before it fully cast. He would probably take a bullet, but with any luck, he might succeed.

But when he made his first step, he felt a vibration through the floor. Before he could take another step, the vibration grew into a strong shake. The shaking intensified as if an earthquake had begun.

Lane cocked her head to the side, looking directly at Max. The gaping hole of her eye socket, dark and wet, dribbled blood down her face. The foul odor of decay oozed across the room.

"Too late," she said and let loose a horrid cackling. "Too late."

Chapter 26

AN EXPLOSIVE FORCE ROCKED THE FOYER. The mark on Max's chest, the curse placed there by Mother Hope, ignited a burning pain straight into his lungs. He had to grab Alan's shoulder to keep from falling over. Loud bangs like dynamite charges rippled from one end of the house to the other. Chelsea covered her ears and curled into a ball at the foot of the stairs. Beneath Lane, the floor cracked along the thick lines of the blood-drawn triangle.

"You see?" she bellowed above the increasing noise. "Aunt Holly always said it only took willpower to overcome these spells. But rare is the witch willing to sacrifice herself."

Another crack in the floor bisected the triangle, forcing Lane to step away. All these fissures widened until the flooring between them fell away, leaving a gap like a large sinkhole. Dust plumed up from beneath.

The rumbling ground, the cracking stone and wood, the booming charges — all of it ceased. Only the echoes remained, diminishing into the distance like a final roll of thunder. The pain in Max's chest also dissipated.

Coughing, Lane waved her hand in front of her face as she peered into the hole. "Alan, I see it. I see the book. Come here. Help me get it out."

As Alan moved, Max saw something he never would have noticed before. His newly-trained martial arts mind recognized that Alan had let his guard down. Acting purely on muscle memory, Max performed a series of self-defense moves he had practiced for months.

His right hand slid down Alan's left arm and clasped the muzzle of the handgun, turning it flat and to the side. At the same time, he pivoted in front of Alan and put all of his weight forward onto the weapon. With his free hand, Max made a fist and punched. Two jabs to the chin were all it took. Pop, pop — and Alan let go of the handgun as he staggered back.

Lane had flattened on the floor with her arm stretching down into the hole. Max pointed the handgun at her.

"Get up, Lane," he said. "It's over, now."

With a flash of the petulant teenager inside, she said, "I gouged out my own eye. You think I care about your little gun? It's not like you're going to shoot me. You're not a murderer."

"I can aim for your leg. You'll live."

She paused, then smiled, and returned to fishing for the book. Max dropped his aim towards her leg. But before he could the pull trigger, Alan tackled him to the ground. The handgun flew out of Max's hand, skidded across the floor, and dropped into the hole.

Max elbowed Alan, connecting with the side of his head. Alan rolled off, clutching his face. When Max scurried back on his feet, Lane had pulled out a leather satchel.

She made sure to stand on the far side of the hole as she unclasped the satchel and opened it. "It's here," she said, blood drooling from her wide-grinning mouth. "It's really here."

It's over, Max thought. All their efforts to stop her had failed. Generations of Dardens casting spells to stop this from happening had failed. And it only took a teenager with the inner-strength to sacrifice an eye. Why Aunt Holly hadn't done that long ago, Max couldn't understand. Everything he had learned about her suggested she had the will for such an act.

Of course, she had to contend with Grandma Darden, and for most of her life she didn't have the hand with the ring. Max halted — *the hand with the ring*. Lane had broken the spells that hid the book and protected it, but without the ring, she could never unlock the power within the book.

Max whirled around and dashed up the stairs, leaping over Chelsea as he went. From below, he heard Lane yell, "He's going for the hand. Stop him!"

At the top of the stairs, he paused, trying to recall if Aunt Holly's bedroom was to the left or the right. He could hear Alan clumping up from behind. No time. Blindly, Max chose left and rushed down the hall.

Every door he saw, he opened. Guest bedrooms, linen closets, one room with a television and a stationary bike — but no Aunt Holly bedroom. He reached the end of the hall. No stairs, no doors. Just a small window overlooking the side yard.

Turning back, he found Alan halfway down the hall. Blood reddened his mouth while sweat soaked his hair and shirt.

"Not looking too good," Max said.

"You know I'm going to have to give you a few whacks to return the favor."

"I figured you might feel that way. But if you're smart, you'll forget about me and go stop your sister. If she opens that book, you'll be lucky if death is the only thing coming your way."

Alan spit to the side, leaving a bloody splotch on the wall. "You think because you spent a few hours doing research that you know us, know our family, know everything about how we live and think. You're more of an idiot than Enrique ever was, and that idiot actually thought he had some way of getting into this family."

"Chelsea seemed to want him." Max tried to relax his

tense muscles as he set his feet in a fighting stance. He tightened his fists.

"It's been a long time since Chelsea had any say in what went on around here. We humor her, that's all." Alan stopped short of being within Max's reach. "Just like I've been humoring you, letting you interview us, making you think you understood the way this family is set up."

"I read the Will. That wasn't made up. You got screwed out of everything — no money, no property, nothing."

Raising his fists, Alan hunched over slightly and added a gentle bounce to his feet. *Like a boxer.* Max had barely gone halfway to his black belt, and Alan appeared to be a seasoned boxer — a lightweight, perhaps out of shape, but a boxer nonetheless. Answering the surprised look on Max's face, Alan said, "Five years off and on. It started as a way to get out the aggression I felt towards Aunt Holly, but it became a real passion."

"I don't suppose you want to back up and let me get by?"

Alan closed in, leading with a jab. The entire move took Max off guard, and Alan caught him in the chin. Max's head rocked back.

"Guess we're done with the banter portion of this fight," Max said.

When Alan jabbed a second time, Max was ready. He blocked from the outside, maintained his balance, and followed up with a counter-punch. But he missed — too slow. Alan scooted out of reach without much effort.

Stuck in the hallway, neither man had enough room to maneuver well. Max hoped it bothered Alan to a greater degree. Alan would be the one who expected to be able to circle an opponent. He would be the one who would know how to take advantage of that. If Max was lucky, his own inexperience might help him in this case by throwing Alan's expectations out the window.

Max attempted to lunge forward, but Alan closed the distance and tossed an uppercut. The jolt to Max's head sent numbing prickles across his entire body. He stumbled back into the wall at the end. No getting lucky with this fight.

If inexperience won't help me, I better think like somebody with a brain. His training taught him that all fighting styles had positive and negative aspects. Alan was a boxer. He would be fast with his hands and be able to charge each punch with great force. He would be light on his feet and good at ducking, dodging, or deflecting punches.

But what about kicks?

When Alan attacked again, Max dropped low and side-kicked at his opponent's shin. He kicked hard, focusing on a target beyond the shin, and heard the bone snap. Alan shouted as he tumbled to the floor.

"Sorry," Max said, gingerly stepping over Alan. He did not feel his kick go all the way through, so while he doubted he broke the leg, he certainly caused a fracture of some sort.

Hurrying back along the hallway, he went by the stairs and started trying doors again. He kept expecting to see Sandra sitting in a circle of chalk and lit candles, but after five doors, he opened the one to Aunt Holly's room. Standing in the hall, he felt a chill prickle his skin.

He glanced down the hall. Alan stood upright and attempted to put weight on his injured leg. He hobbled a step before grabbing at the wall for balance. But he didn't fall. And he took another step. And another.

"Because why should it ever be easy?" Max muttered as he entered the bedroom. At least here, he knew where to look. He opened the walk-in closet — huge and filled with full racks of clothes. Cubbyholes with shoes made up the back wall as well as a full-length mirror. And on a small stool by the shoes, Max saw the cardboard box that held the glass cube.

But it wasn't in there.

He stared at the empty box, his stomach churning, and tried to think. He knew Lane didn't have it — if she did, she would've destroyed everybody by now. Sandra? Maybe she had it. There were still rooms to check.

Bolting out of the bedroom, Max hustled through the hall, checking every remaining door. Alan neared the staircase, but Max didn't see him as a threat anymore — as long as he kept away from Alan's fists. Second to the last door opened on a room with tall windows and the furniture all pushed aside. The circle Sandra had used dominated the floor. But no Sandra.

Did Lane have her? No. If Sandra had the hand and Lane had Sandra, then like before, all would be over. If Lane had Sandra and neither had the hand, then Lane would be calling Max out to come save his wife. Which meant that Lane still had nothing. Plus, Max knew Sandra didn't have the hand because that didn't go with any part of their plan. She wouldn't have abandoned her goal. Not ever. It was too important.

So, where's that damn hand?

Max perked up as he recalled where he last saw it — the library. Chelsea had brought it to him to take a picture. A family this rich would employ a maid. Years of expecting somebody else to clean up a mess would lead to careless behavior. Chelsea probably left the hand in the library knowing that the maid would eventually return it to its rightful place. But since it wasn't in the closet, the maid hadn't done her job yet.

Rushing back into the hall, Max saw Alan had managed to work down several of the stairs. Max dashed forward and tried to use his momentum to carry him through. Alan caught the back of Max's shirt and yanked him off balance. They both fell forward.

Alan barked out as his injured bone fractured more. Max rolled to a stop. He checked over his body — nothing worse than a few bruises. Unless. People died from falling down stairs.

Holding his breath, he reached for the banister. And he touched it. His hand did not go through. He wasn't a ghost. Breathing again, he got back on his feet.

He saw Alan sitting a few steps above, but Alan did not look angry or concerned. Nor did he look like he had given up. Instead, he had a thoughtful gleam in his eye that soon opened into a realization.

Damn. He figured it out.

Alan inhaled deeply and yelled. "Lane! It's in the library!"

Ignoring his bruises, Max raced down the stairs, skipping a few as he went. Chelsea had not moved from the bottom, her back heaving as she wept. Max hurdled over her, then over the hole in the floor, and sprinted toward the library.

He flew through the living room, down another hall, and right by the library doors. He stopped so sharp, he toppled over. Scrambling back, he crashed into the library. Wild-eyed and breathing heavy like a rabid dog, he tried to take in everything at once as if he could single out the glass cube if he only had a complete picture of the room.

Except it wasn't necessary.

Lane had the cube. She stood atop the large desk in the middle of the library. In her right hand, clutched against her chest, she held the original manuscript to *The Malleus Maleficarum*. In her left, she held the glass cube containing the witch Kalinski's petrified hand and the ring. With a mad smile and blood staining her shirt, she watched Max like a victor trying to decide what method of vengeance she would employ upon her enemy.

Then her smile dropped into cold certainty.

Chapter 27

MAX COULD NOT MOVE. It wasn't a spell that kept him frozen to the floor, but rather, fear paralyzed him. He had heard about that happening to people, even had a few instances that came close, but gazing into the eyes of this thing that used to be Lane disconnected his brain from the rest of his body. No matter how he tried, he could not equate the teenage girl he had seen only a short while ago with the monster standing before him.

A loud bang echoed from the foyer, but Max couldn't even flinch. Stretching her sadistic smile wider and wider, Lane opened her hand and let the cube drop. The world slowed down. Max could hear the displaced air as the cube tumbled toward the floor. When it hit, it shattered like a grand ballroom chandelier breaking into thousands of tiny shards.

Lane clasped the book in both hands and held it above the broken glass and the petrified hand. The ancient, dead fingers twitched. At first, Max thought it was moving from the jolt of hitting the floor, but then the fingers all pointed upward at the book. The ring rotated. Over and over. Like a screw being spun loose.

When it finally escaped the hand that held it, the ring lifted into the air. Lane moaned with pleasure as it rose toward the book. Max's breath caught in his chest. He wanted to stop this from happening. If he only could move, he would have gladly rushed forward and tackled Lane to the floor. He would do anything to stop her.

"Max." A deep voice called. "Max, snap out of it."

A pale hand appeared before his face and snapped its fingers. Without moving his head, Max followed the hand to its arm and the arm to its owner — Marshall Drummond.

"C'mon, Max. We gotta get out of here."

"I can't move," he managed.

Drummond snatched a quick look at the ring — less than a foot from the book. "Sorry, pal. I hate when I have to do this to you."

He clutched Max's arm. The icy burn that raced through Max shocked his system. All his muscles contracted in a painful seizure, but it only lasted a second. Drummond immediately let go, and Max collapsed on the floor.

"Now, Max. Run!"

Stumbling blind into the hall like a drunkard barely able to stand, Max dashed toward the foyer. Bright orange light flashed from behind strobing his movements. When he reached the entrance, Sandra rushed towards him and scooped him into her arms.

"It's too late," he said. "I tried to stop her, but I couldn't get the hand. When I saw her in there, I couldn't move."

"We'll be fine," Sandra said. "Sorry it took me so long. Enrique's wards threw Drummond and I out of the house. It took me too long to break back in."

"I love you. I'm sorry for everything I've ever screwed up."

"Stop that. We're not going to die today."

Max buried his head in her shoulder. "You didn't see her. She's going to lay waste to all of us."

"Honey, trust me. We didn't fail."

He raised his head and saw nothing but confidence on Sandra's face. "But —"

"You had to stall long enough for me to cast my spell. And I did it. Look."

She nudged his head to the side. In the doorway, hovering above her wheelchair, Max saw Grandma Darden — clear-eyed and angry.

He managed to stand on his own. "You really did it." He clutched Sandra and kissed her. "You did it!"

Drummond said, "Um, don't mean to break up the celebration, but we haven't won yet."

Grandma Darden floated into the foyer. "The ghost speaks true," she said in a strong, commanding voice. "Get everyone to safety. I'll take care of my granddaughter." She continued to float into the living room and toward the library.

A tremor rumbled the house, and Max's brain kicked back into life. He pointed at Chelsea. "Help get her out of here. I got Alan."

Sandra leaned over Chelsea, murmuring kind words, and aided the weeping lady to her feet. Max went up the stairs. He put Alan's arm over his shoulder.

"This won't be pleasant," he said.

Alan tried to push Max away. "Leave me alone."

Wood splintered and cracks traveled across the walls. "This house is coming down. You need to get out now."

"I'll be fine. Lane will protect me."

"I wouldn't count on that."

Max tried to lift Alan again, but Alan shoved him down two steps. Part of the banister fell off. The sounds of destruction grew louder as the second floor fell apart. Several feet away, Max watched as pieces of the stained-glass dome broke free and burst on the floor like a colorful fireworks display.

Drummond soared through the wall. "Those two witches are about to rain Hellfire on each other. We've got to go."

Calling upon the last of his strength, Max gripped Alan's

shirt and yanked the man toward the exit. But Alan swung his arm over the banister and held tight.

In a soft, low voice, Drummond said, "It's okay. You tried. Some men, when they find out they've been on the wrong side of things, can't deal with that truth. They'll lie to themselves no matter what the cost. As long as they don't have to look in the mirror and see the horror looking back."

"Lane!" Alan cried out. "I'm here!"

Max backed up. Off to his side, plaster dropped from the living room ceiling. He put out his hand to Alan. "Please, come with me."

"You better run. Lane'll rip you to shreds. Lane!"

Lowering his hand and his head, Max said, "I'm sorry." He turned away and walked out of the house.

Chapter 28

SANDRA WAVED MAX AND DRUMMOND OVER to the car parked on the far side of the courtyard. When Max reached the car, he crouched behind the hood. Chelsea sat with her back against the rear tire. She had an empty stare and tear trails running down her cheeks.

They heard a crash of glass and wood. Light flashed in parts of the house — sometimes orange, sometimes green. A window on the second floor blew outward forcing Max and Sandra to duck.

"Anybody got an idea what to do now?" Max said.

Drummond hovered over the car with his hat back and his hands in his pockets. He watched the house crumbling like a spectator at the fair. "Not much we can do," he said. "At least, not until we see who wins. If Grandma is the one standing, then we'll be fine."

"And if it's Lane?"

"Then we need a Plan B. I'm thinking run like hell and don't look back."

Max turned to Sandra. "You got anything more helpful than that?"

"Her power comes from that book," Sandra said. "If we destroy the book —"

"They said it couldn't be destroyed."

"They also said their curses would protect the book. That didn't go so well. I'm not saying it'll be easy, but if it comes to it, I think our choices are destroy the book or Lane destroys us."

As if a bombed building in a warzone, the second floor

of the house collapsed. It fell apart with ease like wood blocks knocked down. "Okay," Max said. "How do we attempt to destroy the book?"

Without moving, Chelsea said, "You can't. It's impossible. When I was younger and I learned about my family legacy, I asked Grandma Darden how to destroy it. I figured if there wasn't a book, there would be no need to become a witch. But she said I wasn't the first in our family to try. As long as there have been Dardens protecting the world from that book, there have been Dardens trying to destroy it. Nobody has ever succeeded."

Drummond said, "My Plan B is starting to sound pretty good."

The outer wall of the living room toppled over. To Max, the resulting crash sounded much like all the others they had heard. Chelsea, however, must have heard something different. She rolled over onto her knees and squinted at the house.

"Enrique?" she said.

Before either Max or Sandra could move, before either could consider that Chelsea might react, Chelsea shot around the car and raced toward Enrique's corpse. Sandra tried to go after her, but Max caught her wrist and pulled her back.

"There's nothing good that'll come from following her," he said.

The classic pillars on the front porch cracked. Jagged pieces slid off, flipped through the air, and smashed on the steps. Finally, one of the pillars gave way. A large chunk near the bottom broke free and the entire pillar crashed through the front door.

From deeper within the house, Max heard a tormented whine. Debris from the fallen second floor erupted into the air along with dust and smoke. Water spewed out of broken pipes. Rising above it all, Lane and Grandma Darden appeared.

Both were bruised and bleeding. Both floated like ghosts. Grandma Darden sped through the air with her hands out like claws. Lane evaded the attack. Grandma Darden spun back with a throwing motion. A green globe of light pitched out at Lane but missed.

Max had never seen magic like this before, and he suspected he never would again. This was not normal witch magic. This was heightened and dark power created by that book. So much power, in fact, Lane could not contain it all, and Grandma Darden had siphoned off some of the energy for herself.

Another green globe soared out from Grandma Darden's hands. Holding the book out like a shield, Lane deflected the magic straight back. It hit Grandma Darden in the chest, launching her into the ground. Lane landed. Her eyes burned with fury as she thrust out her hand. A javelin of orange snapped out and cut into Grandma Darden. Lane then whipped her hand ahead, and Grandma Darden's body slid across the ground, smacking into the side of Max's car.

"She's not moving," Sandra said, her face paling. "I think she's dead."

Max's head bounced up and down. "I'm thinking it's time for Plan B."

He opened the passenger side door, kept low, and crawled into the driver's seat. Sandra came up behind and closed the door. Max dug out his keys and started the car. When he looked up, Lane stood right in front of them.

She placed her free hand on the engine hood. Her mouth moved, but Max could not hear the words. He didn't need to. He knew the look of witchcraft when he saw it. Her hand glowed as it burned into the hood.

Max jammed the car into Drive and floored the gas. But the car did not move. The engine roared and the wheels spun and soon he smelled burning rubber, but they did not move.

"I'm getting stronger," Lane said.

Glancing backwards, Max shifted into Reverse and floored the gas again. Still, the car did not move. Slapping the steering wheel, he put the car in Park and turned it off.

Satisfied, Lane lifted her hand from the hood — a burnt shadow of her hand remained. She glowered at Max and Sandra before brightening with an idea. "I think I'll cook you inside your car. That might be fun. In fact, I'm going to—"

Drummond flashed by as he tackled Lane. His painful screams met with her outraged shock as they slammed into the ground. The book tumbled off to the side.

Throwing open the car door, Max scrabbled across the dirt. The book could only have been a few feet away but it felt like miles. His fingers dug against the rocks and sticks as he propelled closer and closer.

Lane rolled out from under Drummond and reached for the book. Max heard Sandra yell something, and suddenly Drummond endured more pain by locking onto Lane's ankle. Max grabbed the book and backed up against the car. He heard a ding as the ring dislodged from the book and fell.

"I've got it!" Max yelled.

Drummond gratefully let go of Lane. He floated into the air, clutching his stomach and wincing.

Sandra asked, "Are you going to be okay?"

"Never better," he groaned.

"If it makes any difference, it was a nice move."

His clenched lips formed a smile. "I call it Plan C."

The pain Drummond suffered had been equally felt by

Lane. Twice she attempted to stand. Twice she crumpled to her knees.

"Give me the book," she said.

"You've lost," Max said.

"Then die." She thrust her hands out at Max, but nothing happened. She tried again, but still nothing. "Give me the book, now," she said, but it sounded like a whining plea. "I will let you live. I promise."

"You've disgraced your family. You murdered your grandmother and Enrique Cortez. You'll be lucky if the courts let *you* live."

She gazed up at him. "Then I guess I've got nothing to lose."

With a terrible hiss, she planted one foot firm on the ground and shoved hard. But before she could get her other foot up, Chelsea wrapped a hand around Lane's ponytail and wrenched back her neck.

"You foul beast!" Chelsea raised her arm high. Max saw the letter opener in her hand. Dripping with the blood of Enrique, she slammed the letter opener into Lane. Again and again. Into the chest, the neck, the stomach — anywhere her rage brought her hand down. Tears streamed from Chelsea and with each strike she hollered with hoarse weeping. "You destroyed everything!"

She continued stabbing her sister long after Lane ceased moving. When she finally stopped, Chelsea dropped flat on her back and stared at the sky.

The house creaked. Loud snaps of timber followed explosions of stone and marble. Whatever parts of the structure had remained standing finally gave up. With a thunderous crunch, the Darden house collapsed.

Sandra clasped Max's hand. "Come on, hon. We've got to leave here before the police show up."

Chapter 29

Mrs. Porter set the serving tray on the coffee table. She had hot cocoa for PB and J, and coffee for the adults. Max sipped from his mug and eased back on his couch. Sitting in a circle with his family had never felt better.

"I swear, no matter how long I live, I will never understand some people." Mrs. Porter ruffled PB's hair as if to say that she understood him fine.

"It's not that hard," J said. "This Chelsea lady hired us 'cause she didn't like the way her Auntie's Will was set up. She wanted to make trouble for the other kids."

"Yes, but after doing that, why on Earth would she kill everybody? Her sister, her brother, her poor grandmother — all dead. From the news reports, it sounds like she destroyed her home, too. Literally, I mean. Blew the whole thing up with dynamite or something." To Max and Sandra, she added, "You were there. What happened?"

Max choked on his coffee. "Mom, we talked about that. If anybody asks, we were not there. We saw nothing. We left long before Chelsea snapped and did all that horrible stuff."

"Yes, yes, I know. I'm not an idiot. But nobody's asking right now, and I want to know the truth."

"I'm sorry, but that's as much truth as you get to have."

PB patted Mrs. Porter's hand. "You have to get used to that. Some of these cases get a bit classified. Don't worry, though. You find stuff out anyway. Usually it's not all that exciting in the first place."

Later that night, after the boys went home and Mrs.

Porter went to sleep, Max picked up his keys and met Sandra at the front door. "You sure you don't want to come along?" he asked.

She gave him a hug before leaning back in his arms. "It's best if I stay here. That way nobody can find out from me because I won't know where you went. And the way things are right now, I'm guessing that somebody will try to find out."

"It's crazy, isn't it? I thought when we got rid of the Hulls that life would calm down and all this would go away, but it's only gotten worse."

"The Hulls were nasty people but they did create an order to things. Kind of like a mafia boss. You don't like them, but at least they keep the rules clear."

"Now there are no rules."

"Exactly. It's anarchy out there, and whoever grabs enough power will become the witch that makes the new rules."

"We're not going to be done with this, are we? I mean, Drummond's right. No matter what we do, we're responsible to keep up the fight."

Sandra chuckled. "I'll let him know you said he was right."

"Don't you dare."

They kissed again and Max went out to his car. He drove north out of the city, taking Reynolda Road until he saw the branch onto Tobaccoville Road. He parked at the elementary school, shouldered a large supply bag from the trunk, and hiked into the woods.

Drummond was waiting. When Max arrived, Drummond touched the trees and the symbols lit up. Max walked up to the log.

"You sure this is safe?"

Drummond stared at a spot in front of Max's feet.

"Yeah. She's been under there for decades and nobody's seen her. Even those who walk right through here never know. The magic keeps them blind to her presence."

"Okay." From the supply bag, Max pulled out a shovel. He dug into the spot Drummond pointed out. "Should I go all the way down to where she's buried?"

"Maybe not that far. She doesn't have a head, but considering all the things we've seen, she might just be able to grab the book and take its power."

"Not likely. That ring is gone. Besides, Sandra's spell on the book isn't that powerful but it's something, at least. Still, I think I'll stop digging before I reach that witch."

Neither spoke again until Max finished shoveling the dirt back onto the book. As they left the site and Drummond touched the tree marks to set the alarm, Max said, "I hope this doesn't destroy us. It was a curse to the Dardens."

"Yeah, but they were witches. They were tempted by the power they were trying to conceal. You and I aren't going to do anything with that book. I can't even touch it without pain, and you've got no real talent for witchcraft. Not to mention that you can't get to the book without me unlocking the tree wards, so there's no point in comparing us to the Dardens. We're in a much better position to fulfill the job. Trust me. Nobody's getting that book again. Not while you and I are around."

As Max ambled back to the car, Drummond floated by his side. Max said, "It's bugging me that we left Chelsea there."

"Why?" Drummond asked. "She's not innocent in any of this."

"She's not entirely guilty either."

"She killed her sister."

"Okay, she's guilty of that. But the rest of it. I mean,

she's going to be charged with the murder of Enrique and her grandmother."

"All she has to do is tell the truth. She starts spouting off about magic books, curses, and witches, and she won't see a day in prison. They'll send her to a mental ward. Probably a better place for her, and frankly, she could use a little therapy."

Max shrugged. "I suppose."

Drummond stopped and faced Max. "Look, pal, I understand. This was an ugly case, and you're trying to find some silver lining to it all."

"There isn't one, though. If I had acted sooner, maybe all of this wouldn't have happened. Chelsea wouldn't have been charged with multiple counts of murder because if I had acted sooner, it's possible that Enrique would still be alive."

"You can't go living your life wondering *if.* That way leads to real madness. Besides, you helped stop a crazy teen from killing a lot of folks, and you helped Chelsea survive. Not bad things to chalk up."

"I know."

Snapping his fingers, he said, "Hey, you want the real silver lining to this case? I got it for you."

"What?"

"We got paid. In full, in advance."

Max laughed. "Okay, you win."

They returned to Max's car and drove back home.

Afterword

If you're reading this, chances are you've already read the whole book. For that, I thank you. As these books have grown in popularity, my appreciation for you readers deepens, too. It amazes me that you all enjoy reading about Max and the gang as much as I enjoy writing about them. As always, if you keep reading these books, I'll keep writing them! Without further delay, though, here's the stuff you really want to know:

The tale of the Spaghetti Man is true — all of it except for Edith Walker's involvement which is entirely my creation. But the petrified man, the tourist attraction it became, and the interference from an Italian politician all happened. Also true is that the story made it on the CBS News. A quick YouTube search should bring up the broadcast for those of you who want to see. I discovered this bizarre story while researching for *Southern Curses* and knew that someday I'd find a reason to put it in a Max Porter novel. Thankfully, that time has come.

The murder of Alexander Simpson by his child-bride, the poorly executed arsenic plan, the court case, and the involvement of a fortune teller named Polly Rising is also true. All the details, names, and conversations surrounding the murder are also true. The only liberties I took were in suggesting that Ms. Rising was a witch with ulterior motives and that she went on to live an unnaturally long life.

Finally, *The Malleus Maleficarum* is a real book about witch hunting and has been referred to by many as the most evil book ever written. There is plenty of information online about the book including a simple Wikipedia article to get you started down that rabbit hole. To the best of my knowledge, there are neither secret spells surrounding this book nor are there secret covens hiding the book from being read. But the existence of the book is true as well as the numerous women who were hunted down, tortured, drowned, or burned at the stake under the false belief that they were magical and malicious beings of evil.

The Dardens, their plantation home, and all of their family history derive purely from my imagination.

Acknowledgements

There never ceases to be people to thank for the creation of each novel. More and more, those people don't even know they contributed because it did not come through anything directly related, but rather, they gave an encouraging word, a nuanced view, or in some other way redirected my thoughts that eventually led to this book being better. Two of those people are John Hartness and Dean Wesley Smith. I've known John for years and I've never met Dean, but in a short span of time, both men helped me realize that I am, in the best sense of the word, a pulp writer. That has helped me focus my writing and my art toward the things I love most about telling stories.

Of course, I must thank Claudia Ianniciello for another awesome cover. Working with Claudia has been a joyful experience, and I can't wait to see what she comes up with next. My unwavering thanks to Lisa Gall, Toni Shepard, and the rest of my Launch Team. You all give these books (and my ego) the boost we need to keep this series going. And naturally, to Glory and Gabe.

But my eternal thanks is always left for you, my readers. Nothing a writer creates is ever fully-formed until those words are read. Because of you, I keep getting to create more and more. Thank you for that privilege.

About the Author

Stuart Jaffe is the madman behind *The Max Porter Paranormal Mysteries,* the *Nathan K* thrillers, *The Malja Chronicles, The Bluesman, Founders, Real Magic,* and so much more. His unique brand of old pulp adventure mixed with a contemporary sensibility brings out the best in a variety of SF/F sub-genres. He trained in martial arts for over a decade until a knee injury ended that practice. Now, he plays lead guitar in a local blues band, *The Bootleggers,* and enjoys life on a small farm in rural North Carolina. For those who continue to keep count, the animal list is as follows: one dog, two cats, three aquatic turtles, seven chickens, and a horse. As best as he's been able to manage, Stuart has made sure that the chickens and the horse do not live in the house.

Don't miss Max's next great mystery!

Max Porter has had his share of odd cases. That goes with the territory when one of your partners is the ghost of a 1940s detective. But the idea of being hired by a witch coven to save witches seems wrong from the start, and it only gets worse.

Bad enough that Max can't trust anything his clients say, but his own wife is being lured closer into becoming a real witch — something that terrifies Max and sows distrust. Add to that a mysterious group of witch hunters, a long dead curse brought back to cause havoc, and power players in the shadows, and it's no wonder The Porter Agency is stretched to the breaking point.

Between fighting their enemies and fighting each other, this may end up the toughest case of their lives. One that could alter the balance of power among all witches for years to come.

AVAILABLE NOW!

Be sure to check out the thrilling Nathan K series!

IMMORTAL KILLERS

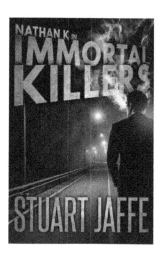

Nathan Flynn is trying to get a start in life - law school, internship, and a fiancé. But when he finds himself on the wrong end of a knife, everything changes. He should have died. Instead, he acquires a unique ability - he harbors two souls in his body. If he dies, he loses one soul yet continues on. As long as he replenishes his second soul, he cannot be killed - he's immortal.

But gaining immortality throws him into a world of government spies, crime syndicate couriers, and elite assassins. A world in which mankind is second class. A world where one has all eternity to master anything, and he is not the only one.

Nathan wants nothing to do with such a dangerous world. He wants to help people, not destroy them. But when he tries to leave, he learns that freedom will be a lot harder to gain than he thinks.

Catch up with Max Porter!

From ancient curses to witch covens, World War II secrets to local lore, underground boxing to underground chambers, Max Porter and his team investigate it all.

Don't miss a single story in the bestselling series, the Max Porter Paranormal Mysteries.

Made in the USA
Las Vegas, NV
17 September 2022

55473345R00132